body check

Boston Grizzlies Hockey Club
Book Two

allie lasky

boston grizzlies hockey club

Reading Order

Here is the recommended reading order for this series:

Tending Her Heart (Seb and Audrey)

Puck Me Twice (Sven and Vanessa)

Home for the Holidays (Jake and Rachel)

Body Check (Jason and Amelia)

Defenseless (Ryan and Hailey)

Power Play (Al and Riley)

Game Misconduct (Nick and Bex)

Instigator (Aidan and Ceci)

One Timer (Adam and Avery)

Delay of Game (Parker and Ivy)

one

. . .

Amelia

IT'S two o'clock in the morning, and the neighbor whose window faces mine has their lights on. Day or night, the lights are always on. I'm not sure if the apartment is vacant or still being renovated. I only know that when my curtains are open, like they are every night, the glow from the other unit casts gentle warmth into my apartment, more soothing than a nightlight.

But I've never seen a person over there before.

The baby cries and I lurch out of bed, plodding my way across the hallway. As I reach Ainsley's door, my brother barrels out of his room and into the next, a bottle in his hand. From the doorway, I watch as he picks up his newborn daughter and snuggles her, soothing her cries. In short order, her snuffles die down as she gulps down her milk, and I can rest easy, knowing she's taken care of.

Returning to my room, I notice movement throughout the window. There's a dark figure in the apartment across from mine, illuminated by the bright, yellow lights.

Male. Tall. Broad.

A shiver runs down my spine when I realize I'm only wearing a tank top and undies.

And it's not until he crosses his arms over his chest, attention clearly focused on my window, that I realize he can see me.

All of me.

For some reason, that terrifies me and exhilarates me at the same time. I don't know him from Adam. He could be an investment banker or an insurance salesman or a serial killer, for all I know.

The distance between us and the poor lighting hides his features, but there's no mistaking the burn of his gaze on me. How long has he been standing there? How much has he seen?

I should close my curtains. Now that I know someone lives there, I should cover up and retain my last bit of privacy before it's stripped away.

Too bad I like being watched.

And it's not like he's looking away. No, his gaze is intent on my barely clothed body, burning me up inside. I don't need to see his face to know he's looking at me, and that he likes what he sees. If he didn't, he wouldn't be watching.

Crawling into bed, I expect him to turn away. His eyes are locked on me as I kick back the sheets. I reach for the bedside drawer, pulling out a toy.

Am I really doing this?

The man braces a thick forearm on the balcony's glass door, his attention locked on me.

Peeling off my tank top and panties, I lay naked in bed, guiding the toy between my legs and turning it on. The vibration increases as I twist up the intensity until my nipples pebble into tight buds and my back arches.

My eyes drift across the way to my neighbor, shrouded in the dark of night, highlighted by the lights behind him.

He doesn't look away.

He's shirtless, a pair of sweatpants riding low on his hips. Even from here, I can tell he's in shape. Athletic. A broad chest leads to a narrow waist, and although I can't see definition from here, I'd bet dollars to donuts he's built.

My eyes fall closed and I force them open, back to him. His inscrutable gaze is locked on me, on the toy disappearing between my legs, on the way I'm riding it.

Wishing it was a man surging inside of me and not silicone.

Wanting more. *Needing* more.

I play with my breasts, tugging and pinching my nipples. Heat coils low in my belly, but it's not enough. My head lolls to the side as I watch my neighbor.

And then his hand slides down his muscular chest to the waistband of his sweats. His hand doesn't dive inside; not yet. He seems content to let this play out.

Touching myself, I drive the toy between my legs, letting my hips ride the silicone. Everything inside of me burns white-hot, the fire in my core threatening to overtake me.

When he finally slips his hand inside his pants, touching himself, *allowing* himself to let go, I shatter.

I shatter into a thousand, million pieces, splintering apart and coming back together anew.

My pussy clenches around the silicone, wringing every last scrap of pleasure from the toy, and as I turn off the vibration and pull it from inside me, his heavy gaze burns into mine.

I don't know him. But I know what he likes.

Watching me.

His arm moves faster now, the balcony hiding his lower body from me.

But he's breathing harder, and his arm shifts with every stroke.

And *something* splashes onto his bare chest before he sags onto the balcony door.

What will he do next?

The stranger pushes off the patio door, grabbing a nearby

something—a rag, or maybe a t-shirt, or a towel—and wiping the cum from his chest. His gaze is locks on me, his expression inscrutable.

Lifting a hand, I give him an awkward wave.

His entire body goes still. I bet he even stops breathing. *Does he think I can't see him?*

Finally, he shakes his head, scrubbing a hand over his face before turning away. Then, with a long, last look over his shoulder, he turns out the lights.

I lay naked and sweating in bed, thoroughly spent. Curling onto my side, I pull the blankets over my shoulders and try to sleep.

I don't close the curtains.

But the next night, his apartment is dark.

two

. . .

Jason

I **FEEL** like I'm eighteen again, constantly beating off to the memory of my new neighbor putting on a show for me.

Because it was a show. There's no denying she knew I was there. She knew I was watching, and she did it anyway.

And while I'd normally feel guilty about perving on a younger woman in a vulnerable position… there's nothing about our encounter that indicated she wasn't fully consenting.

Fuck, and I don't even know her name. More importantly, I don't know her apartment number. I'm sure I could reverse engineer what floor she lives on—it's the same level as mine, and I'm on the nineteenth floor—but her building probably has a different unit system than mine.

It's early, maybe five o'clock in the morning. The team plane has just landed at the airfield, and I'm trudging into my apartment when movement in place catches my attention.

Except it's not the woman who haunted my dreams for the last week.

There's a man in the apartment across from mine, shirtless, a tiny baby snuggled in his arms. He's bouncing the baby, his lips moving as he says something.

As if he senses me watching, the man pauses, and then his eyes trail across the way. He lifts a hand in greeting and turns his back, still rocking the baby.

And then I see her. In the early morning light, she's wearing tight shorts and a loose top. Her dark hair is cut bluntly just beneath her shoulders. She hands the man a bottle, but doesn't move to take the baby.

She has a baby.

I perved on a woman who has a baby. And a partner.

Fuck. I'm just as depraved as my ex-wife always said.

Leaving my suitcase in the middle of my apartment, I strip out of my clothes and crash into bed. When I wake up a few hours later, everything hurts.

As I stumble to the bathroom, I glance to the left, to my open bedroom window. I forgot to close the blinds, too exhausted to care.

There's nobody in the apartment across the way. Good. I'll make sure to close the blinds going forward. We're strangers; we don't need intimate access to each other's lives.

Guilt churns in my stomach at the memory of the woman, naked and wanting. The way I wanted to leap from my apartment to hers and take the invitation, to kiss her lips, to lick my way down her body, to taste her pussy. The show she put on was for me, and we both know it.

Her face was shrouded in shadow, so even if I ran into her on the street, I can't guarantee that I'd recognize her features. But I know her body. I know what she looks like in the throes of pleasure.

I know I want to watch her again, and again, and again.

But she has a partner. A baby. I can't take advantage of her. I don't condone cheating, especially after the way my marriage broke up.

Shaking my head, I push the thoughts aside, and focus on the here and now. I've got a workout in half an hour, then film review, and a meeting with Coach and the front office.

Being captain of an Original Six hockey team is not for the faint of heart. It's a grueling job, even more intense than actually playing hockey. I'm the liaison between the team and the staff, and everyone wants a piece of me. That's not me being conceited; it's fact. Between my teammates wanting advice on their shots or bending my ear about their girl problems, and the coaching staff griping about specific players' faults, and management wanting a impossibly long list of social media access, it never ends.

When my marriage fell apart, it was almost a relief. I didn't have to keep placating Harper with promises we both knew I'd never be able to fulfill. The team comes first. It has to.

The drive to the practice facility is over before I know it, and as I make my way past the security desk with a wave to Joe, the old security guard, the familiar hum of activity soothes that itch in my soul.

I missed this.

The off-season was long, and although we're still in preseason prep mode, I don't feel like I'm all the way back yet. We've played three games—one home, two away—and have another five on our schedule before the regular season starts.

Between the divorce finalizing, the renovations on my new condo, and finally moving in last week, I've barely able to relax all summer. My only vacation was a week at the lake house with my parents, my siblings, and their children. And let me just say, no matter how many hours you spend in a beach chair on the lakefront, it's not a vacation when you're woken up each morning before five o'clock by three screaming toddlers and *Bluey* blasting on the TV.

I love my siblings. I love my nieces and nephews. I just love them more from a distance.

Maybe it'll be different with my own kids. Harper didn't want them, and I was ambivalent, so we never tried. Guess that's a good thing with the way everything worked out. For now, I have to give hockey and the team my focus. I don't have any space for anyone else.

"Morning, McKittrick," Coach Turner says as I enter the players' lounge. He's pouring coffee into a thermos. "Rest well?"

My laugh is as bitter as the black coffee he's drinking. "Not exactly."

We got home from the airport in shortly before dawn, but even though I slept hard, I'm not rested. Not after realizing my mysterious temptress has a family of her own.

He frowns. "Your knee still giving you trouble?"

"I'm fine." Last season, I had some twinges in my knee after a bad hit, but with a few injections and some physical therapy, I played the rest of the season.

The doctor cleared me at my pre-season physical. I'm in tip-top shape.

Coach sighs. "If something's up, I'd rather get it straightened out now, before we start the full campaign. Swing by Derek's. He'll sort you out."

He's the team's athletic trainer. We're very well acquainted with one another.

"Yes, Coach."

It's not a request, it's an order, and I recognize it.

Two guys come barreling into the lounge. Al Gonzales, better known as Gonzo, is a burly bear with a heart of gold. His sister hangs out with the team a lot, and I've heard her refer to him as a golden retriever, whatever that means. I guess he is kind of dopey, like a dog. And a damn good hockey player, too.

Beside him is Ryan Logan, a defenseman who gives off major *don't fuck with me* vibes. Off the ice, he's sweet as a kitten; when there's a skirmish on the ice, he's not afraid to use his claws. He's generally a decent guy. Quiet. Keeps to himself.

Walking sedately behind the two idiots is Aidan MacGregor, one of my alternate captains. He's also the center on my line. His face is permanently set into a scowl. The only things that can bring a smile to his face are his sister, Hailey, or video games.

He's the type of nerd who brings a gaming console on the road, but he always invites the other guys to play with him, so it's not like he's *completely* anti-social. He's not into the bar scene, which I can respect. We have enough difficulty with other players getting into their cups the night before a game, but I've never had to worry about MacGregor overindulging.

Logan gives me a nod as he grabs a bottle of water from the drinks fridge. We have a separate fridge for snacks and another for ready-made meals we can heat and eat. And that doesn't include the catering trays the chef whips up on the regular. The Grizzlies work hard to take good care of us, making sure our every need is met.

All they ask is that we win some hockey games. Maybe bring home the Stanley Cup. Totally doable, right?

three

· · ·

Amelia

MY HEAD SPINS AS DEREK, my new boss, takes me on a tour of the training facility. So far, the Boston Grizzlies' layout doesn't look all that different from the Colorado Dragons' lair I recently left. Hallways are different, the suite of exam rooms is on a different offshoot from the main dressing room, but for the most part, once you've been in the bowels of a few training facilities, they all start to look alike.

We make our way through the dressing room and down another hallway before entering a bright, airy lounge. There are floor-to-ceiling windows illuminating the space, a selection of couches and armchairs, a ping-pong table, assorted tables and chairs, and three refrigerators.

"This is where the players hang out most," Derek says, sweeping his arm wide. "You can take breaks in here if you'd like, but the food is reserved for the players."

"Got it." I didn't expect them to feed me. All I need is a place to fill up my water bottle and a place to store my lunch bag, and I'm good.

There are a few players in the lounge. They look over at us with interest.

The guy on the left is a bearded, burly beast of a man. He

nods, his eyes doing little to disguise his curiosity. The man beside him, dark-skinned with a short beard and kind eyes, glances at me and immediately returns to peeling an orange. The redhead cocks his head, studying me for a second, before he shakes his head and then returns to their conversation.

But it's the man in the center of the lounge who catches my attention.

He's tall, maybe the tallest in the room. His light brown hair looks soft, and his short scruff highlights his square jaw. His eyes, though—they're wide, unblinking, and he's staring at me with horror on his face.

What's his deal?

Blinking a few times, I focus on Derek again.

"This is Amelia. She's joining our team as a physical therapist," my boss says. "Please help her feel welcome with us."

"Nice to meet you," the redhead says. "I'm MacGregor."

"Forward," I reply.

His face scrunches. "I'm not making a pass at you. I'm—"

"You're a forward. That's the position you play." I roll my lips inward to hide my smile. "You're primarily a center, right? Though sometimes you play on the left wing. Never the right."

Chin hitching up, he stares at me through narrowed eyes. "How do you know that?"

"I have a dossier on each player. And you have a history of left ankle issues." Cocking my head, I study him. He's a ball of tightly coiled tension. "Don't worry. We'll make sure we're keeping you in excellent shape."

MacGregor nods tightly.

The dark-skinned man beside him laughs. "I'm Logan."

"Defenseman. Paired with Pope last season." He signed with Washington during the free agency period.

"And good riddance," MacGregor mutters.

My eyebrows go up.

"We've got a good group of guys this season," Logan says. "We shouldn't have any more issues."

"Right. Well, we'll make sure your hip is taken care of."

"Shit, how do you *do* that?" The bearded, burly guy says in wonder. "I'm Gonzales. Most guys call me—"

"Gonzo," I finish.

"Yeah. Did you memorize the files or something?"

Shrugging, I try to downplay it. "I studied."

It's not like I've been able to do much else. My seven-week-old niece, Ainsley, is adorable, but she only sleeps if someone holds her. I've spent a lot of time with her strapped to my chest as I vacuum or wash dishes or study. Noise doesn't bother her, thank goodness, but as soon as I stop moving, she starts shrieking.

Was I planning on moving cross-country, living with my brother and his husband, and starting a new job seven weeks after giving birth? No. Am I going to make the most of it? Absolutely.

I look over at the last man. There's something familiar about him, but I've already looked over the roster, and there aren't any players who were part of the Dragons or the Austin organizations.

I was lucky to intern with the Austin Aces while I finished up my DPT degree, and after two and a half seasons with Colorado, I was ready to move on. Luckily, the Grizzlies were hiring, and one of my brother's exes works for the team, so I networked my way into an interview.

I earned this job on my own fucking merit, though, and I won't let anyone tell me otherwise. Sports in general, and hockey in particular, are a good ol' boys' club, and it all comes down to who you know. I won't stand for anyone insinuating I didn't get this job fair and square, simply because Robby put in a reference for me.

Speaking of… The assistant equipment manager enters the lounge, a bright smile stretching his face. His dark blond hair is styled away from his eyes, highlighting his strong features. He's always been attractive; I can see why my brother fell for him all those years ago.

"Hey, Meels." He squeezes my shoulder. "So glad to have you here."

"Thanks, Robby. Happy to be here."

The last man in the room—the one who stared at me with the horror on his face—scoffs. Now, he looks between me and Robby with undisguised interest.

"You all better be on your best behavior for Amelia," Robby says sternly. "Or I'll make sure your blades are extra dull."

I glare at him. "You don't need to threaten them. I'm sure they'll learn I'm scary enough on my own. And they don't need dull blades. That's a surefire way for them to wind up on my exam table."

He laughs. "Yes, ma'am." He nods at the unnamed man. "McKittrick, do you have some time to review the work orders?"

Jason McKittrick. The team captain. He's thirty-seven and nursing more injuries than anyone else on the team. Name a body part and he's probably tweaked it. That's what happens when a guy competes at the highest level of the sport for nearly twenty years, plus a lifetime of hockey before that.

McKittrick's eyes hold no warmth as he glares at me. "Yeah, that's fine." He addresses Robby, though his eyes are locked on me. "I'm available."

Derek clears his throat. "Right. Well, we should get on with the tour."

We continue through the facility. I meet the administrative staff, the logistics team, the coach, and GM. There are players in the hallways, too—Seb Henry, one of the goaltenders, Adam Sinclair, a defenseman, and Parker Jenkins, a young forward in his second year with the organization.

Everyone is polite. Everyone treats me with respect. It's the bare minimum, but it's refreshing nonetheless.

Derek and I return to the medical wing, where we'll spend most of our time. There are three physical therapists on staff, plus him as the head athletic trainer. We have a row of cubicles, where we can sit to enter notes and review treatment plans. He has an actual office with a desk and a door. Rounding out our space are the four private exam rooms, where we treat players before and after games.

Next door is the team doctor's space, where Dr. Hudson can stitch the players back together, take x-rays, and start IVs when needed. There's even a dental suite where Dr. Kerrigan does emergency dental work, if called upon.

I make it through my first day with little issue. There's no game tonight, so I shadow Derek while he works on Larsson's ankle and Sinclair's wrist. He lets me take the lead on Reynolds' shoulder, and we work together on Jenkins' elbow.

At five o'clock, there's a knock on the open door to the treatment room, where I'm organizing supplies.

"Hey, Meels," Robby says. "How's the first day?"

"Pretty good." I'm respected and supported by Derek and the rest of the team. "You?"

"I'm great. Want to grab a drink?"

I pause. I should get home, relieve Tyler and Brandon, and let them have some much-needed time alone. On the other hand, it's my night with Ainsley, and I need all the relaxation I can get before another sleepless night.

"Sure. Where're we going?" I ask.

"There's a pub nearby we like." He takes my jacket off the hook by the door, holding it open for me.

"You don't have to flatter me," I tease. "I'm not going to sleep with you."

Robby's loud laugh catches the attention of some passing players. Including, I notice, McKittrick.

"Trust me, babe, you're not my type."

"I know your type," I taunt back. "Still scarred by it, in fact."

He dated my brother for a year and a half, but given how many times I walked in on them naked in the small apartment Ty and I shared in Austin… Suffice to say, I've seen enough of my brother's bare ass.

Not that he and Brandon are any better at keeping their bedroom activities confined to the bedroom. I think it's a fault of Tyler's, and not necessarily his partners.

Never did I think I'd share an exhibitionism kink with my brother. Just the thought makes me gag.

"Come on," Robby says, sliding his hand into mine. "I want to hear about everything you've been up to."

four

. . .

Jason

I DON'T LIKE THIS.

Amelia, my gorgeous new neighbor, is basically on a date with Robby Andrews. Doesn't he know she has a family at home?

They're sitting close together at a table in the bar, each sipping a beer. As she talks, Amelia twirls her hair around her finger, a bright smile on her face. Andrews laughs, throwing his head back, and her satisfied smirk makes my stomach twist.

How do they know each other?

Gonzo and Logan sit across from me at a four-top, my seat giving me the perfect line of sight to Amelia's table.

She works for the team.

She's even more gorgeous up close. Her eyes are a rich, chocolate brown, her skin bronzed with the vestiges of a warm, summer tan. The impetuous shape of her mouth painted in dark red lipstick sends my heartrate into overdrive. And the way she rattled off each players' ailments... Fuck, I got hard in the middle of the players' lounge, watching her dress down each of my teammates.

And now she's on a date with Andrews. Doesn't she know the team frowns on fraternization?

There's a relationship declaration form that has to be filed with HR. When Larsson and Vanessa, our logistics coordinator, first got together last season, it caused a storm in the dressing room. Everyone likes Vanessa. We don't want her to go anywhere.

But then Larsson announced everything was aboveboard, that they'd already filed the form with HR, and everyone breathed a sigh of relief. They're engaged now. I don't think she's leaving the team anytime soon.

"What's your deal?" Gonzo asks as the waiter sets a new beer in front of me.

"What do you mean?"

"You asked us to grab a drink, but you've spent the last twenty minutes glaring at the new PT. What's going on?"

With a sigh, I shake my head and take a pull on my beer. "Just distracted."

"Dick-stracted?" he taunts.

I roll my eyes. "No. I've never met her before today."

"Oh, so it's a lust at first sight situation," Logan says, with a knowing nod.

"Fuck off. It's not like that."

"Then what's it like?" he asks.

"It's... I don't know." Running my hand through my hair, I search for words that won't come. "I honestly don't know."

Gonzo chews on his lip. "Have you gone out?"

"What do you mean?"

"Since everything was finalized with Harper. Have you gone out and gotten your dick wet?"

Wincing at the crude words, I know there's no way out of this. "Not yet."

"Well, what are you waiting for?" Gonzo demands.

"Hey, if he's not ready, he's not ready," Logan says.

"Thanks," I bite out.

"It can't be easy starting over at his advanced age," he finishes.

"Oh, fuck off." I take a drag on my beer. "I'm not that old."

"Nine years older than me," the bastard says, with a grin.

Rolling my eyes, I turn it back around on him. "So, when will you ask Hailey out?"

Logan scowls. "Fuck off."

"What, my sister isn't good enough for you?" Gonzo chimes in. "You have to go after MacGregor's sister?"

"I'm not going after anyone's sister, because I'm not going after *anyone*," Logan grits out. "Hailey and I are just friends."

Logan and MacGregor went to high school together. They're both from the same small town in Wisconsin. Logan signed with Boston last summer after a few seasons with Minnesota, and MacGregor's been a mainstay on our first line for years.

He thinks we don't know it, but everyone sees the way Logan moons after Hailey MacGregor. His best friend's little sister. Like that won't blow up in all of their faces.

"How is Cari doing?" I ask Gonzo. His sister graduated from college last spring. "She plays rugby, right?"

"With the Revolution," he confirms. That's the city's women's rugby team. He signed a three-year deal with the Grizzlies at the start of the summer, bringing him back to his hometown. "Their season starts in the spring."

"Well, we'll have to go to a game," I decide, making a mental note. "Send her schedule to Vanessa in logistics, and she'll make sure we show up to support her."

"Thanks, man. That would be great."

"This team is a family. We all support each other."

Gonzo grins. "Well, I'm currently living in my childhood bedroom, so I've had it up to here with family."

"You're staying with your parents?" Logan asks.

"Well, my parents' house. They live in Florida to take care of my *abuela*. My brother and sister live there, too." Gonzo shudders. "I thought about getting a place of my own, but it's not like we're home that much during the season."

"True," I reply. Harper hated how frequently we traveled. No matter how many years we were together, she never understood the demands of a professional hockey career. She wanted the galas and vacations; she didn't want to be there for the slog of back-to-back games and road trips.

I know it's a good thing we got divorced. We were simply incompatible, but I don't know how to reconcile the life I thought I had with the life I still have ahead of me. I had this picture of how everything would turn out, and now I have to toss it all away. Start fresh.

My eyes flicker across the bar to where Amelia and Andrews are talking. His hand is on her arm now.

Is he making a pass at her? On her first day, no less?

Before I know what's happening, I stalk across the bar to their table.

"McKittrick," Amelia says with a smile, nodding at me. "What can we do for you?"

My eyes narrow as I stare her down. "There's a non-fraternization policy with this team."

"Oh? Does that mean I can't grab a drink with a coworker?" Her eyes drift across the bar to my table. "Does that mean you can't hang out with your teammates outside of the arena?"

"What? No. Of course not."

"Then why does it matter if an old friend and I grab a drink after our workday?" She cocks her head at me. "Do you interrogate every new hire?"

"No."

But she's not simply another new hire. She's my showgirl.

"What, exactly, is your problem with me?"

"You are."

Her glare sharpens. "Because I'm a woman in a man's job?"

"Don't you have a family at home?"

"Because I have a uterus, I automatically am not complete if I don't have a child?" The scathing look sends chills up my spine. "Fuck you, McKittrick. I thought you were different."

This is going all wrong.

"Because I saw you with your baby!" I burst out.

Her eyes widen. "What the hell are you talking about?"

"My apartment faces yours. I saw you—" I clamp my lips. *Fuck.* I wasn't supposed to say that.

But I also couldn't let her go on without knowing. I saw her intimately, in a way that she probably wouldn't want her coworker to see her.

"You saw me?" The blood drains from her face.

And now she knows *exactly* how much I saw.

"Yeah. You and your husband. I notice you're not wearing a ring, though."

Amelia blinks a few times. "I'm not married. I live with my brother."

Andrews coughs to cover a laugh. Rounding on him, he meets the full force of my glare with a pissed off scowl of his own.

"But—the baby—"

"My niece," she says tightly.

Scrubbing at my forehead, I try to make it make sense. It doesn't.

"I don't get it."

"Ainsley is my brother's daughter," she says slowly. "We're all living together, one big happy family."

"Why?"

Her laugh is incredulous, on the border of manic. "Because rent is fucking expensive, because my brother has a newborn, because my other brother travels three quarters of the year. Because I have nobody in this city, I'm starting over, and I needed a fucking break. *Fuck.*"

"Hey," Andrews cuts in. "You have me. I'm on your side."

"I know. I appreciate you, more than I can possibly say." Amelia smiles at him, but when she turns back to me, the sharp glare is back. "Did I pass your interrogation?"

There's no saving this. No coming back from this.

With a curt nod, I turn on my heel and walk out of the bar.

five

. . .

Amelia

JASON MCKITTRICK IS MY NEIGHBOR. The captain of
the team I work for saw me naked, watched me get myself
off, touched himself while I put on a show for him.

Fuck. What a way to start a new job.

When I get home from the bar, Tyler and Brandon are
eating dinner. I'd texted them not to wait for me, and Robby
and I ended up getting some appetizers, but watching them
dive into a Katsu curry makes my stomach growl. The air is
fragrant with the familiar perfume of spices. It reminds me of
home, of the two years we were stationed in Okinawa when I
was in elementary school.

"We saved you a plate," Brandon says, kicking out a chair.

"You didn't have to do that," I mutter as I drop my
lunchbox off on the kitchen counter and fall into the empty
chair.

"Wanted to," my brother-in-law says. "How was work?"

"Fine."

"Robby didn't give you any issues?" Tyler asks.

"Nah, he took me out for a drink after. It's nice to have a
friendly face around." Spooning the curry on my plate, I meet

my brother-in-law's eyes. "It isn't weird for you? Me talking about him?"

Brandon shakes his head. "I know Ty has a past. I also know he's committed to me and our family. Would it be strange if Rob suddenly hung around? Maybe. But I would never ask you to give up on a friendship, especially now."

Now that I have nobody.

"Thanks, Brando."

His lips tip up and he pushes the bowl of rice toward me. "You look hungry."

In other words, he's done talking about this.

The baby squawks, and I set down my fork before crossing the room to the bassinet.

"Are you feeling left out, baby girl?" I coo as I lift my niece into my arms. She squirms in my hold, her mouth puckering.

"I'll grab a bottle," Tyler says, standing from the table.

When my brother and his husband announced they were thinking about adopting, I asked if they considered surrogacy. They had. But the waiting lists, and finding a donor egg... It was all too much, especially with Brando was about to leave for spring training.

For reasons I still don't fully understand, I volunteered. I donated my eggs to them, fertilized in a lab with Brandon's sperm, and carried my niece, giving birth to her seven weeks ago.

There isn't anything I wouldn't do for my brother. Giving him a baby, something he couldn't give his husband? Yeah, I volunteered in a heartbeat, and when they're ready for another kid in a few years, I'll do it again.

It was a hell of a battle to get a doctor to agree to the surrogacy. Most of the time, they will only allow women who've carried their own children to term to do it. But with an extensive psychological evaluation, plus my insistence that I don't want any kids of my own, we finally found a doctor to to go along with the plan.

Also, I get to stay close to the baby I carried for nine months, the baby I knew as well as my own heartbeat. This is the closest I'll come to being a mother. Most days, I'm perfectly content with that.

It's hard to have kids with the career I chose. As long as I work in professional sports, I'll travel for eight months of the year, if not more. If I go the clinic route, I'd have more stability, but I wouldn't work the kinds of cases that most interest me. I'm consciously making the decision to put my career first, and I'm genuinely happy with that choice.

It's all hypothetical, anyway. I'm not anywhere close to settling down. My career is just getting started; I'm not about to hamstring myself this early on.

Even if... Bitterly, I glare at the apartment across from ours. The lights are on in McKittrick's apartment, but he's nowhere to be found.

I don't know what happened to him after he left the bar. In the midst of our conversation, he turned around and left. Just like that.

Taking the bottle from Tyler, I feed my niece, enjoying the simple pleasure of caring for her needs. There isn't much I can offer her. I don't know the first thing about being a mother or an aunt. I didn't have either growing up.

What I can do is love her, teach her right from wrong, support her unconditionally, and give her a safe space when her dads drive her up the wall.

All the things I wanted as a kid and never had.

It's not my dad's fault; he meant well. He was just... limited. Stunted. I see him a few times a year, but we aren't close. Not like Ty and I are.

Trauma-bonded. That's what my last therapist called it. Tyler and I are in sync on a deeper level than most siblings.

Nobody else knows what we went through. Nobody else can really comprehend it.

We've always lived together. He's only a year older than me, so he took a gap year, and we went to the University of Illinois together. When I was accepted into my DPT program in Austin, he came with me. One afternoon, he stopped by the clinic where I was interning, and he met Brando, a college baseball player who was on my table. Their whirlwind romance was the stuff of storybooks.

They've been together four years next month. Married for two and a half. When Brandon signed with Boston, they moved here, and I went to Colorado for a fresh start with my shiny, new Doctor of Physical Therapy degree.

It didn't last long. As soon as my second full season ended, the Dragons essentially told me not to come back after my maternity leave was over, and I moved to Boston to be with my brothers. No regrets.

Brandon tried to get me a gig with the Bulldogs, but they were all set with their staff. I was planning to start a job search after I recovered from the birth, so when Robby called me with the Grizzlies' job opening, I jumped at the chance. After interning with the Austin Aces, I knew I wanted to work with athletes, and hockey players in particular.

After Ainsley finishes her bottle, Brandon takes his daughter and burps her, then settles her in the carrier and straps her to his chest. I finish eating my dinner, Tyler keeping me company.

He bumps my foot with his under the table. "It wasn't so bad, was it?"

"Hm?"

"Your first day. It was okay?"

"Up until…" With a sigh, I shake my head.

"What?"

"I don't want to get into it. What did you do today?"

"Meels, tell me." Tyler pokes my side. "Did something happen?"

"Turns out the team captain is our neighbor." I jerk my head toward the brightly lit window facing ours. There's still no sign of McKittrick. "He thought you were my husband."

"Gross." My brother's face scrunches with disgust. "Marrying a woman. Blegh."

Brandon laughs. "So, it's gross that she's a woman, not that she's your sister?"

Now, both Tyler and I gag.

"Don't be nasty," he chides his husband.

Ainsley squawks as if in agreement, and the three of us laugh.

Ty and I work together to put away the leftovers and clean the kitchen, and then the three of them settle in to watch TV.

"Do you want me to take her?" I offer, silently hoping they say no.

Brandon grins. "You've already got her tonight. We're good for now."

We take the night shift in turns. The guys have two nights each a week to my one, and on my turn, they usually go out for a date and grown-up alone time. It helps fight off the newborn exhaustion. Everyone should have a three person co-parenting situation like ours.

Eventually, I'll have to move out and move on with my life. I can't live in Tyler's apartment forever. Who knows where Brandon will get traded, and if I'll hold down this job any better than the last one.

Besides, I signed a legal document giving up all rights to Ainsley. She belongs to Ty and Brandon. I would never try to take their daughter away from her rightful fathers.

It's only the postpartum hormones making me hyperfixate on everything wrong or scary in my life. The doctors warned me it could take a while for everything to settle, especially living here with the three of them. They're a family unit, and I'm outside of that.

For now, I have some downtime, so I draw a bubble bath and find a good book on my Kindle. A nice soak in the giant tub is exactly what I need to set myself back to rights. With the help of a few candles and my favorite hot cocoa soap, I feel almost like myself again. My hair is piled in a messy bun on the top of my head, and I applied a clay mask to my face.

I can do this. I can do anything I set my mind to.

When the water runs cool, I drain the tub and get out. Wrapping a towel around my body, I plod back to my room in my robe and bunny slippers. I start to drop the towel when my eyes flicker to the open curtains.

There's a man in the window, and he's staring right at me.

McKittrick.

He doesn't look away, doesn't concede defeat.

I drop the towel.

six

. . .

Jason

THIS IS SO WRONG.

Amelia stares at me with defiance in her eyes as she drops her towel, baring her nude form to me. I should look away. I should be the bigger person. We have to *work* together.

But as my eyes drink in the sight of her, the dips and curves of her body, her rounded belly, her full breasts... The flush high in her cheeks, the brightness in her eyes...

She likes this.

She likes being watched.

And fuck, do I ever like watching.

My gaze roves over her delicious body, memorizing each and every inch. What I would give for us to be alone in the same room, to devour her the way I've wanted to ever since her first *show* for me nine days ago.

It's torture knowing it can never happen, not if we're working together. Not to mention the supreme awkwardness of sleeping with my neighbor. What if it doesn't go well? We'd still have to see each other, and then we wouldn't even have the privacy of the workday to distance ourselves.

No. This can't happen. I should put a stop to it. Right... now.

Or now.

Or… maybe tomorrow.

Amelia turns, offering me a glimpse of her backside as she looks over her shoulder at me. Her hair is in a messy knot on the top of her head. I want to pull the tie out, watch it cascade over her shoulders. Want to grip her hips with my hands, to cup her ass and knead it. Maybe smack it a few times. It's rounded and full, and I bet it would give a good jiggle if I fucked her from behind.

Fuck. This is so wrong.

She's a team employee. We work together. She'll be putting her hands on my body…

My cock kicks, lengthening against my thigh in my joggers, and still, I can't look away. I'll have to ask Derek to take care of my aches and pains from now on. There's only one ache I want her to handle, and it's the one in my cock.

It's so much worse knowing who she is. Before, I could chalk it up to an accident, a one-time thing. I never had to see her again.

Now…

Amelia turns around, giving me a full-frontal view of the most beautiful body I've ever seen. Her chin lifts, her eyes locked on mine as she trails her fingertips over her breasts and down her rounded belly to the apex of her thighs. She touches herself, practically daring me to do the same.

I'm going to hell. Book me a one-way ticket because I'm out of here.

Slipping my hand into my pants, I stroke my cock to full hardness, and then pull myself out. I don't think she can see me—my balcony has a half-wall, offering me a specter of privacy—but I'm certain she knows I'm touching myself, watching her touch herself. Taking advantage of the pleasure she's so freely offering. She has to know. She wouldn't be doing this if she didn't want me to.

Will she still meet my eyes in the cold light of day? Will *I* be able to meet hers?

I'm fixated on the sight of her, the pebbled tips of her nipples, the way her fingers disappear into her cunt. Even though I can't see it, I know she's slick and wet, ready for me. I wonder what she tastes like, what she would feel like if my fingers pushed inside her, the sounds I'd rip from her throat while I pleasured her.

My fist works over my cock, the tip leaking pre-cum like a geyser. The stickiness helps my hand glide over my length, but it's not enough. I want more.

I want *her*.

Across the way, Amelia's mouth drops open as her fingers work her pretty pink clit. But she doesn't look away. Her gaze locks on mine while she brings herself to the brink.

Come for me.

Her body tenses, and then I watch from too far away as she lets out a groan I wish I could hear. She bites down on her lip—hard, I can tell—as her body wracks with pleasure.

I want to be the one tearing her apart. I want to be the one putting her back together.

Lightning travels down my spine, and my balls draw up high and tight. That's all the warning I have before my orgasm barrels through me. I come into my fist, my moans stifled by the windows separating us.

Amelia holds up her hand to me, fingers wet with her juices.

Huffing out a laugh, I hold up my hand too, showing her the cum streaking my palm.

She grins, making a motion as if to high-five me. I shake my head, a smile crossing my face. This woman. What am I going to do with her?

She opens a nearby door—an en suite, maybe?—and disappears, returning a few minutes later, still naked as the day she was born. She pulls out her hair tie, shaking the strands loose, before tying it up again in a more secure knot. She turns off the main ceiling light, and the only glow in the room is a soft lamp on the nightstand.

I can't look away as she picks up a tablet or e-reader, and then climbs into bed. She glances back at me—still with my pants down, cum drying on my hand—and gives me a smile and a wave.

Dismissing me.

Kicking off my sweats, I trudge to the bathroom and clean myself up, too. I take a hot shower, throw on a new pair of sweats, and then collapse onto my bed to watch ESPN. Every few moments, I glance over at her window, at the soft glow of her bedside lamp, and the blue light from her e-reader.

Eventually, I look over and the lights are out. She's fast asleep, the covers pulled up over her shoulders. I have the inexplicable urge to kiss her forehead. I don't know this woman, not really, not outside of our two incredibly intimate encounters. Watching her sleep is like an invitation to intimacy I haven't earned.

But I don't close my blinds.

seven

. . .

Amelia

WORK SETTLES INTO A ROUTINE. This is my third hockey team; I've got the basics down. Each morning, I meet with Derek, the head athletic trainer, Dr. Hudson, the team orthopedist, and Trevor, the rehabilitation director, plus the two other PTs, Zac and Graham.

Is it unnerving being the only female on the team? A little. But I grew up with a single father and a brother. I've always thrived in male-dominated environments, and I'm not about to let something as simple as *nerves* get in my way. If it takes sheer spite to succeed in this world, by damn, I'll do it.

We go over the known injuries on the team, the things we're watching out for, and Trevor gives us directions. For the most part, I have flexibility to assign my patients exercises, but all the PTs have to run our long-term treatment plans past him. It's not personal, even if being micro-managed rankles. At least it's all three of us and not just me being singled out.

Dr. Hudson heads back to his clinic—he comes in for our daily meeting, and then examines anyone who needs seeing to before returning to his daily gig. Trevor goes back to his desk. Derek divvies up the caseload between me, Zac, and Graham.

Larsson is usually my first patient of the day. His right ankle is bugging him, and he likes to get it worked on before morning skate, and then focus on strength training and recovery. He can skate through the pain, but it still needs a bit of attention.

The quiet Swede is a joy to work on. He flinches when I touch him, so I make sure to warm my hands first, and then he does the exercises I select without griping. If only all my patients were as amenable as him.

After Larsson, my morning is a flurry of activity. Reynolds, Jenkins, and Sinclair all get treatments, and I'm just typing up the notes on Henry's shoulder when there's a knock on the door. Zac is on the ice with MacGregor and Graham is taking a coffee break, so I'm alone for once.

"Hm?" I glance over my shoulder at the noise, and then freeze.

Jason McKittrick is in the doorway, a stricken look on his face. For such a bold man, I'm surprised he's so skittish around me.

"How can I help you?" I ask, putting aside my work tablet.

"My, uh, knee. It's sore."

"Hop on up." I pat the exam table, pulling a fresh sheet of paper over it, and then grab a new pair of gloves.

McKittrick looks at me, then at the table, and then back to me. "I don't think that's a good idea. I can wait for someone else."

Hands on my hips, I glare at him. "Do you have a problem with me working on you?"

His throat bobs as he swallows. "No?"

"Because it seems like you do."

"I don't," he says quickly. "It's only…"

"What?" *Is this because he's seen me naked?*

"I don't want to make you uncomfortable," he finally says.

"Right now, you're just pissing me off," I mutter under my

breath. I pat the table again. "Come on, let me work out your issue and get you on your way."

And out of my way.

He grunts as he steps up onto the table, stretching out. Even with our extra-long exam tables, he hangs off the edge. After all, he is the tallest player on the team at six-foot-six.

I start with a visual inspection. The skin isn't broken or bruised; no acute injury. Leading with a soft tissue massage, I palpate the knee, watching his face closely for any hint of pain.

McKittrick grimaces when I touch him, and instead of backing off, I go deeper. His soft grunt gives me immense satisfaction.

"It's your osteoarthritis," I tell him. "We can get it straightened out."

"Great. Awesome," he grunts, as I continue to stimulate the area. "How about now?"

Finishing my exam, I offer him a hand, and he swings into an upright position. I take a seat on my stool and pick up my tablet, flicking to his file.

"You've had four surgeries on that knee."

"Well, one was in high school," he says. "Does it still count?"

"Yes, even last century still counts," I tease.

He makes a face. "I'm not old."

"Didn't say you were." Although the streaks of gray in his hair do lend him a distinguished air.

"You're just a child." He scowls, as if personally offended.

"I'm twenty-seven." Not that my age has anything to do with him.

His swallow echoes loudly. "Fuck."

"Are we going to talk about how old you are? Because at thirty-seven—"

"I'm far from the oldest player in the league. There are guys five years older than me still playing," McKittrick says with a petulant scowl, as if the expressions makes him seem younger.

There are three players over forty in the league. A few more in their late thirties. They're an anomaly, not the norm.

"You're the oldest player on this team." I shrug. "I'm not complaining, though. You should play as long as you're able. And if we take care of your knee, I don't see why you can't have another few seasons."

"Few." He turns the word over, distaste clear on his features. "Not five. Not ten. A few."

"Nobody's career is guaranteed. I don't have a crystal ball. How many more seasons is up to you and your agent. But we can work together to keep you in shape, to keep your knee performing at its best."

Slowly, he nods. "Okay."

"Good. Let's get to work."

We focus on stabilizing his knee and doing some stretching exercises. He's a fairly good sport, all things considered. His earlier hesitation with me aside, I think we can work together. Maybe. Possibly.

If I don't give in to tearing off his clothes first.

This job means too much to me to throw it all away on a casual fuck. I don't get lasting, forever vibes from McKittrick. He's too focused on hockey. He's too focused on the here and now. He's not ready for a future.

And frankly, me neither. I'm only twenty-seven. I have enough on my plate, starting over in a brand new city with no friends, aside from my brother and his husband. I love them dearly, but they're fuckheads. And they're starting their own family. They don't need me crashing in their apartment. They deserve to start their own life without me in it.

Even if the thought of more distance from Tyler anymore makes me want to curl up in a ball and cry. Brandon never makes me feel less than for needing my big brother. If anything, he supports me and encourages my relationship with Tyler. He really is the best possible partner for my brother. I couldn't be happier that the two of them get their happily ever after.

Even if it means I probably need to find a new place to live.

For now, though, I'll focus on work. I'll make new friends, even if I have to go outside my comfort zone. I can totally make new friends. I've done it before. I'm sure I'll have to do it again. I can do hard things. That's the story of my life, isn't it? We all have to do hard things.

McKittrick won't meet my eyes as I help him stretch his hamstring. He lets out a satisfying grunt when I press on the back of his leg, testing his mobility. It's an incredibly intimate position, me leaning on his leg, pressing into his body. Our faces are close, his breath puffing on my lips. But then I hit that point, the angle that gets to him, and he lets out a sigh, going pliant. He gives in. He submits.

He might not submit in any other aspect of his life, but here on my table, I'm the one in control. I'm the one in charge. And I fucking love it.

eight

. . .

Jason

THE TEAM JET is decked out in black and gold. The boys are buoyant tonight after a 3-1 win over Carolina. We're off on a three game road trip to the Midwest. This is the best time of year to hit Detroit, Chicago, and St. Louis. I'd much rather go in October than February.

Amelia is at the back of the plane with Zac and Derek. Graham stayed home with the injured players, working on their recoveries. I never paid attention to the physical therapists' rotation before.

I overheard Trevor, the director of rehabilitation, talking about how they switch shifts so that one person is always home and the other two get to travel. Zac has young kids, but he's also been on road trips in the past. It helps to have a deep enough bench that you can rotate. I know all about that approach. I do it every day on the ice.

In the first three weeks of the season, I notice Amelia everywhere. It's like I can't escape her. Every morning, I wake up, and I see her empty bed. When I go to sleep, it's only after checking on her, asleep in her own bed, to make sure she's okay. I don't know why she doesn't draw her curtains, but I can't bring myself to close my blinds, either.

There haven't been any more shows or glimpses. At work, we keep things strictly PG. Not even PG-13. It's all completely aboveboard.

So, why do I hate it so fucking much?

I watch her brother with the baby. Occasionally, there's another man with him. I rarely see the three of them together. I feel like I should go over and introduce myself. After all, I stare into their apartment every night. Still, what her brothers don't know won't hurt them. The last thing I need is to get in a fistfight with those clowns, thinking I'm taking advantage of their very much consenting little sister.

At least, I think she's a little sister. She could be the older one. I don't get that vibe, though.

There's something about Amelia that says she's a scrappy little fighter, the kind that stuck up for herself as a kid. Not that her brother wouldn't protect her. More like, it was the two of them against the world.

I want to get to know her. I want to learn what makes her tick. And fuck, do I ever want to watch her fuck her fingers again.

But I don't get to. I don't have that right. We're coworkers and nothing more. I'm not cut out for a relationship, and it is a supremely terrible idea to fuck around at work.

Especially as a captain. The team counts on me to hold myself accountable, to set a good example. I can't do that if I'm screwing the staff.

Even if our first time together occurred before she joined the team. It doesn't matter. I have to hold myself to a higher standard.

Our flight lands, and two buses arrive to bring us to the hotel. One bus is reserved for players and coaching staff, the other for support staff. I don't usually pay attention to who gets on which bus.

But then, Amelia steps onto our bus, and everything goes fuzzy. She sits in the front with Zac, three rows ahead of me on the opposite aisle. Her dark hair is pulled into a ponytail, showcasing the long column of her neck. What I would give to bury my face there, to lick and suck at her sensitive skin.

It's the middle of the night. That's why everything is suddenly on fire, why my cock surges in the confines of my suit pants. I'm sleep-deprived. When I get to the hotel, I'll rub one out and hopefully crash.

Except when we get to the hotel and receive our room keys, she's in the elevator, too. I can't escape her. Somehow, she ends up right in front of me, and when Jenkins climbs aboard, she moves back, nearly stepping on my toes to give him room. Her back is plastered to my front, her ass brushing against the tops of my thighs. She's nearly a foot shorter than me, which means she's average height.

Even after working the game and then the flight, I can still smell a hint of her perfume. Something sweet. It's not over-powering, not like the stench of the other guys' colognes in the tight confines of the elevator. The subtle scent of hot cocoa and marshmallows washes over me, settling the nervous churning in my gut.

The elevator chimes, the doors open on the fifth floor, and all the guys pour out.

"You coming, Cap?" Sinclair asks, holding his arm between the doors.

"Nah, I'm on seven," I tell him. "Goodnight. Get some sleep."

"You, too," the defenseman says. "'Night, Amelia."

"Goodnight," she says. Exhaustion colors her voice, and when the last person files out, she moves away from me.

"So, you're on seven, too?" I ask, trying (and failing) to keep my voice neutral. Instead, it comes out rough as gravel.

"I'm on eight," she says, without looking at me.

I let out a soft hum. "Too bad."

She glares at me, and then lets out a loud, long yawn. "Why is it too bad?"

"I don't know. I kind of like being neighbors."

Does she put on a show for everyone in the neighborhood, or am I the lucky one?

Her eyes flash. "You—"

The elevator chimes when we reach the seventh floor.

"Have a good night, Amelia." I tip my head when I squeeze past her. What I'd give to brush my body against hers, to finally feel her beneath me as I—

Exhaling slowly, I look over my shoulder, but the elevator already closed, whisking her away. With a sigh, I trudge down the hallway until I reach my impersonal hotel room.

Kicking off my shoes, I pull at the knot in my tie, and then strip off my shirt and pants. I should probably hang up the suit, but right now, I can't be bothered.

My pulse is thready, heat circling in my gut as my semi turns into a full-blown erection. Her scent is in my nose, furling through me, like a wisp of smoke curling off a fire. I stroke myself, my eyes falling shut as her image appears on the backs of my eyelids. Her lithe body, the rounded swells of her breasts, her full hips and the swell of her belly… Her fingers delving between her legs, coming out slick…

A groan falls from my lips as I work my cock, wishing Amelia was standing before me. My imagination conjures up an image of her falling to her knees, taking me in her slim hand, her lips stretched wide around my cock.

My breaths come faster now, my hand jerking my cock as if my life depends on it. I want her to knock on my door, to barge into my room and offer to *take care* of me.

Next time I'm on her table, maybe her hand will move from my knee to my thigh, and then higher…

Electricity travels down my spine, a clear warning sign, and I come with a long, rattly groan. Cum fills my fist, and I'm aware of sweat prickling my skin. Fuck. I need another shower.

But it's Amelia I'm thinking about while I clean up. Wishing our relationship was real and not simply a fantasy.

Shit. I've got to get this under control. I can't keep lusting after a team employee. My neighbor. A woman ten years younger…

No. This is not okay. This pesky attraction to her needs to go away—and fast.

nine

. . .

Amelia

THE BOYS ARE in a good mood as we pile into the seedy dive bar they selected for the night. This is my fourth road trip with the team, and whenever we have a night off, the guys inevitably end up in a bar.

The Grizzlies tend to prefer casual bars and pubs versus the swanky clubs the Colorado boys liked. I didn't travel enough with the Aces as an intern to get a pulse on what they were into.

Robby and I are seated at a table with Patrice, the social media guru, and Vanessa, the logistics coordinator. Zac, Derek, and Trevor are shooting pool, but after spending all day with them, I don't see the need to be attached at the hip during our down time.

Joaquin, the team's videographer, approaches with a pitcher of beer and a stack of cups. "First round's on Larsson," he announces, and Vanessa goes red.

Sven's her fiancé. They're absolutely adorable together.

"I'm surprised you two aren't canoodling in a corner," Patrice teases her.

"There's still time, don't count her out yet," Robby grins.

He pours a beer for her, but she waves him off. "You're not drinking?"

She shakes her head. "Not tonight."

Patrice's eyes narrow in thought. "You didn't drink during the last road trip, either."

"I'm pregnant," Vanessa says, with a shrug.

Robby's jaw drops. "You're pregnant?"

She tenses. "Yes?"

To all of our surprise, he launches around the table and pulls her into a hug.

"Nessie! I'm so happy for you!" His eyes are squeezed shut, but I notice a tear slipping free. "You're really doing it. You're making your own family."

"Yeah. Well…" Vanessa clears her throat. "I told Jacky, but not the rest of the guys yet. Sven doesn't want a big announcement."

"Okay, but what do *you* want?" Joaquin asks. "We could do a gender reveal and each of the guys hit a puck with pink or blue powder inside. I could put it on the team's social media."

"Have you thought about endorsements? I can see Sven pushing a high-end stroller," Patrice adds.

Vanessa shakes her head. "I'm not ready to think of all that. I have six more months before I have to worry about it."

"Those months pass by quicker than you think," I warn her. "One minute, you're worried about starting to show, and then two minutes later, you can't zip your jeans anymore."

"You have kids?" Joaquin asks.

"I was a surrogate for my brother and his husband." Taking a sip of my beer, I shrug. "If you need advice or just want to talk about being pregnant, I'm happy to chat. I'm here for you."

"Thanks, Amelia," Vanessa says, her eyes bright. "I appreciate that. None of my friends have kids or even thought about it, and I don't have any family. I'm a little out of my element."

"We all are, at first." I reach out and squeeze her hand. "You're going to rock being a mom."

Robby, still standing, comes around and hugs me, too. "I'm so fucking proud of you," he murmurs in my ear.

We spent a lot of time together during the eighteen months he dated my brother, but after the break-up, we all went our separate ways. Then, he started working for the Grizzlies two seasons ago, and I saw him when our teams played each other. We grabbed coffee or had dinner when we were in the same city once or twice a year. He's a good guy, and just because things fizzled out with my brother doesn't mean we can't be friends. Especially now that we work together.

There's a strict divide between players and staff. Even now, the guys are separate from the rest of us. A few of them are chatting up women, but the majority of them cluster together, chatting and drinking. This isn't an official team event, so attendance isn't required. Still, seventeen of the twenty-three players on this road trip are here at the bar, and most of the support staff is, too.

McKittrick is at a table with Larsson, Logan, and Gonzo, but his attention is on his whiskey. Even from across the room, I can tell he's had a few.

"What's his deal?" I ask Robby, nodding toward the team's captain, who's now swaying in his seat. "Does he typically get wasted the night before a game?"

My friend looks over his shoulder at the table, and then curses. "No. Definitely atypical."

"Guess he's taking the divorce pretty hard," Patrice says.

"He's married?" I can't keep the incredulity out of my voice. That fucker stood there and watched me, and all the while he's *married* to another woman…

"The divorce was finalized in the off-season," Joaquin tells me. "His ex was a total see-you-next-Tuesday." He hiccups and his cheeks flush as he covers his mouth with a wink. "I didn't say that."

"You're not on camera," Patrice says, patting his hand.

"No, only behind it." He goes to drink his beer, but Robby pulls it away and shoves a bottle of water into his hand. "I don't want this."

"Too bad. Drink it anyway." There's a hint of steel in his voice.

"Ooh, yes Daddy," Joaquin says, and all of us crack up, Robby most of all.

Our loud laughter draws the attention of the nearby tables. McKittrick looks up, his eyes narrowing on us.

On me.

A flare of heat rushes through me, warming me from the inside out. All of my nerves stand at attention, ready and waiting.

Fuck. Letting out a shallow breath, I push my chair back, the wood scraping the floor.

"I need some air," I announce. "Be right back."

Making my way through the crowd, I use the restroom and wash my hands. Staring at me in the mirror is a face I hardly recognize. My cheeks are flushed, my eyes bright and wild. And my hair—I don't even know what's going on with it.

Splashing some cool water on my face, I finger-comb my hair back into place. Satisfied I look presentable again, I open the bathroom door.

Only to run smack into a brick wall.

Wait, it's not a wall. It's a chest.

A very hard, muscular chest.

Jason McKittrick stares at me with confusion on his face. "What're you doing in the men's room?"

"This isn't the men's room."

He scoffs. "'Course it is."

Taking his the elbow, I lead him from the cramped restroom. "Come on. Let's get you some water."

"I'm fine. Not drunk," he insists.

"I didn't say you were."

Except he's weaving on his feet, his gait unsteady. He's two hundred twenty pounds of solid muscle. There's no way I can catch him when he undoubtedly falls.

Robby and Joaquin spot us, looking between themselves, before they both spring to their feet and rush over to us.

"Come on, Cap," Joaquin says, diving under one of McKittrick's arms. "We've got you."

"Just needa piss," the hockey player slurs.

Chuckling under his breath, Robby takes my place, swooping in to support his other side. "We'll help you."

"Don't need you to hold my dick."

"Wasn't offering to," Robby snaps back.

Together, the three of them lumber toward the men's room at the back of the hallway. When they come out a good five minutes later, I offer the bottle of water I grabbed from the bar.

"Drink this," I instruct, and McKittrick blinks at me blearily. With a sigh, I wrench open the top and hand it back to him.

With a shaky hand, he takes the bottle and slurps at it, spilling some down his shirt.

"Shit," Joaquin breathes. "He's a mess."

"Coach is already back at the hotel," Robby says. "How're we going to get him past the front door?"

"The service entrance." It's the only way Coach—or by the reporters who hang out in the hotel bar—won't see him.

"So, you're volunteering?" he asks.

Making a face, I sigh. "If I have to."

"I'll settle the tab," Joaquin offers.

"Thanks, man." Robby offers him a fist-bump.

He disappears, and I slide myself onto McKittrick's right

side again. Joaquin returns a few moments later with my purse, and all three of our jackets. Given the heat radiating off the hockey player, I doubt I'll need it.

Luckily, the hotel is only two blocks away—no need for a ride-share.

"Do you want to tell me what this is about?" Robby asks as we shuffle along the street.

"'S nothing," McKittrick slurs. "I'm fine."

"You sure look fine," I snark at him.

He scowls. "You look *fine*." But he sings the word, drawing it out. If his eyes weren't half-closed, I'd say he was leering, but he looks constipated more than anything.

Robby snickers. "He'll regret this."

"Hopefully, he won't remember it."

Our progress is slow but steady. The hotel security guard laughs as we make our way to the service entrance, but they let us through. I punch the elevator for the seventh floor.

"Where's his key?" I ask. McKittrick is even more out of it, staring off into space without a care in the world.

Robby shrugs. "Probably his wallet."

"Okay, so get it."

His eyebrows go up. "You think he wants a gay guy putting a hand into his pocket?"

"He's not that insecure." But I shift and shove my hand into the front pocket of his pants, pulling out his wallet. There's some cash, a half dozen cards, and a condom tucked inside, but no room key.

I blow out a breath. "Fine. Take him to my room."

"You sure about that?" Doubt is written clear across his face. "If it gets out…"

"Well, it's your room or mine. Either way, our reputation is shit." I've never looked twice at a player. Hell, I've never even looked *once*. And somehow, this asshole has me risking my job for—what? A peep show?

"We'll get him settled in your room, and then you can bunk with me," Robby offers. "I have two fulls in my room."

"Sounds good." We lumber up to the eighth floor, and I scan my key, gaining entry to the small hotel room.

Dumping McKittrick unceremoniously on the bed, Robby takes off his shoes while I pack a bag with the essentials I'll need for an overnight stay.

"Ready to go?" he asks.

"Don't go," the hockey player slurs. "Don't wanna be alone."

Glancing at Robby, I ask a silent question, and he shrugs.

"In for a penny, in for a pound," he says.

With a sigh, I sink onto the armchair. "Okay. I'll stay."

My friend bustles around the room, procuring another water bottle and some Advil. He stops and kisses my forehead.

"You're a good egg, Meels," he says, before he leaves.

McKittrick thrashes in the bed. I make my way over and run my hand through his hair, letting the soft strands sift through my fingers.

He whines, a needy noise deep in the back of his throat. I start to pull away, and his big hand wraps around my wrist, his grip firm.

"Don't," he says, his eyes closed. "Don't stop."

I run my finger through his hair again and again, scratching at the back of his scalp, fluffing the strands of hair, massaging his head until he drifts off.

When he lets out a snore, I step back, and when he doesn't jerk, I slowly back away and return to the armchair.

Hopefully, when he wakes up, he won't remember any of this.

ten

. . .

Jason

THERE'S a woman in the bed beside me.

What the fuck did I do?

My head pounds and my mouth is drier than the Sahara, but all I can think about is the soft, warm body spooning me from behind. I never get to be the little spoon; I'm always the big spoon, whether I like it or not.

There's an arm slung around my waist, the fingernails painted a soft pink color. Who do I know that wears pink nail polish?

My head throbs and my bladder protests, so I ease out of the bed and lumber to the bathroom to take care of business. Washing my hands, I splash some cold water on my face, taking in the cosmetics bag on the bathroom counter and the bra hanging on the hook behind the door. It's pink and lacy. I'm definitely not in my room.

There's no sign of a condom wrapper in the trash. Fuck. I hope we were safe. Although I'm still wearing my jeans, there's no dried cum in my pubes, and given the extent of my hangover, I highly doubt I cleaned myself up properly afterward, so…

Maybe we didn't have sex?

Lurching back to the main room, I spot the pills on the bedside table and swallow them, chasing them down with a gulp of water. My eyes are dry from having slept in my contacts, but as my bed partner turns and her hair falls to the side, there's no denying what I'm seeing.

I slept with Amelia Owen.

I'm in Amelia Owen's hotel room.

She's wearing a pair of soft-looking flannel pajamas, the red and black buffalo check in stark relief against the crisp, white sheets. Her dark hair is in a pink silk scrunchie, exposing her face and the long column of her neck. Fuck, she's gorgeous.

This is bad. Very, very bad.

She shifts in the bed, making a soft noise deep in her throat. Her face scrunches, as if something is wrong, and I have the inexplicable urge to rub away the crease between her brows. What can possibly be bothering her?

I need to get out of here—and fast.

My shoes are placed at the side of the desk. Stumbling, I manage to get them on, and then slide my wallet and phone into my pockets. The hotel room key is in the back of the case, right where I left it.

Making a swift escape, I take the stairs down one floor to my room. There's a housekeeper in uniform pushing a laundry cart, and she nods at me when I pass by.

Inside the room, I chug another bottle of water. It's early—we don't have to leave for morning skate for another two hours—but I'm wide awake, so I throw myself into the shower, shave, and dress in casual clothes. My headache has mostly receded by the time I make it downstairs.

The team rents out a meeting room for meals and activities, and I arrive as the catering dishes are being set out. I grab a plate and fill it up, my stomach simultaneously growling and protesting the sight of food.

Coach Turner is nursing his coffee, eggs and bacon on a plate beside a grapefruit.

"Morning, Coach," I greet. We're the only two in the room. It would be awkward to ignore him.

"Morning," he grunts. He eyes me curiously, no doubt clocking the bags under my eyes. "You're up early."

"Couldn't sleep."

He hums under his breath, stabbing at the grapefruit. "Let Doc know if you need to take something."

"I'm fine for tonight. I'll take a pre-game nap and make up for it."

I'm sure I'll sleep better without Amelia sharing the bed with me.

Fuck. How the hell did I end up in her bed?

The last thing I remember is drinking at the bar. She was at a table with some of the other staffers—including Andrews. Fucking Andrews. Is she fucking Andrews?

My stomach roils. I have no claim to her. I'm only her neighbor. But I don't like the idea of her hooking up with some other dude.

Forcing myself to eat, I make it through the meal without being sick. Guys filter in, looking markedly better than I feel. MacGregor and Logan nod as they sit at the other end of my table.

"You okay, man?" Logan asks quietly.

I arch an eyebrow in his direction.

"You were pretty messed up last night," he says.

"I'm fine."

MacGregor hums. "Okay. But if you're not, that's okay, too. It must be hard, getting back out there."

"It's not a big deal." Bringing the coffee cup to my lips, I prepare to take a sip when Amelia walks in, Andrews on her heels. I choke on the steaming hot liquid, my throat scalded.

"Shit, dude," Gonzo says, slapping me on the back. I have no idea where he came from. "Breathe."

"I'm okay," I mutter, wiping my face with a napkin.

"What happened?" he asks, flopping into the seat beside mine.

"Swallowed funny."

He gives me an odd look. "Yeah, okay. Sure."

Unfortunately, the commotion attracted attention, and I'm aware of everyone's eyes on me.

Everyone, that is, except for Amelia and Andrews. They're off in la la land, completely oblivious, as he hands her a plate at the buffet line. She smiles at him, the expression so unlike the scowl she aims my way.

Why does she like him?

And, more importantly, why doesn't she like *me*?

Do I even *want* her to like me? We're only neighbors; I don't particularly like my other neighbors. Fuck, I don't know most of their names. Even in the house Harper and I shared for five and a half years, I didn't make friends with anyone outside of those immediately next door to us. And I wouldn't say I *made friends* with them, per se, but we were amicable and chatted over the backyard fence line.

Since I moved into my condo the week before preseason started, I haven't been home long enough to talk to anyone I don't already know. Eight other players live in the building. It's part of the reason why I chose that building over any other in the city.

Given that I'm in the last year of my contract, I could have gotten a one-year lease, but that felt like tempting fate. Like if I didn't put down roots, there wouldn't be an opportunity to do so later. Who knows where I'll be this time next year? Hopefully, I'll still be with Boston, still playing the game I love.

But I'm all too aware this could all be gone in the blink of an eye. Fourteen years in the big leagues, two in the minors, three of college hockey, two of juniors, and a lifetime more before that.

I'm not ready to be done. I sacrificed my marriage to play hockey. I'm not ready to give it up yet. I don't know if I'll ever be.

Sooner or later, hockey will be done with me—whether I'm ready or not.

eleven

. . .

Amelia

"THIS IS SO EXCITING," Tyler says as he looks around the facility.

"Don't embarrass me," I tell him. "Please."

Brandon slings his arm around my shoulders, baby Ainsley strapped to his chest. "Don't worry, Meels. We've got you."

Shaking my head, I mutter, "Yeah, that's what I'm afraid of."

The arena is aflutter with pre-game activity. I've already clocked out for the day, but it's hard to leave work knowing the guys are about to go head-to-head with Ottawa in ninety short minutes.

"Well, look who the cat dragged in," Robby says loudly, and a few guys turn to look as the assistant equipment manager approaches us. He gives Tyler a broad grin. "Hey, Ty. Brando."

"Rob. Good to see you," my brother says, offering his hand. "You're looking good."

"You, too." Robby turns his attention to the baby, his finger running over her tiny fist. "And who's this?"

"This is our daughter," Brandon says. "Ainsley."

I swear Robby's heart melts right in front of us. "Shit, she's gorgeous." He winks at me, and then grins at Brando. "You guys look good with a kid. Total Daddies."

Ty snickers, elbowing his husband. "We're Daddies now."

"You're annoying now," I mutter under my breath. Except it isn't quite as quiet as I hoped.

Gonzo, ten feet away at his cubby, laughs. "This must be your family."

With a sigh, I resign myself to an inquisition. "This is my brother, Tyler, and his husband, Brandon."

"Nice to meet you, man," Gonzo says, standing and walking over on his skate blades. His hockey pants are loose around the waist, and as he waddles over, they slip dangerously low on his hips. He grabs at them, and then offers his hand for a shake. "Al Gonzales. We love Amelia here."

My face flushes. "Shut up."

My brother laughs. "You just have to stand there and take it. Let them praise you."

"That's not my kink."

Brandon chokes out a laugh. "Yeah, I don't need to know my baby sister's kinks."

I roll my eyes. "I stopped being your baby sister the second they implanted me with your sperm."

Tyler gags. "We don't need any more incest jokes, thanks."

Gonzo's eyes ping back and forth between us. "You guys are hilarious. Reminds me of my siblings."

"Do people also make incestuous jokes about you and your siblings?" I ask, cocking my head.

He snickers. "No. Not a chance."

Robby grins. "This is so much more fun than I thought."

"So, you all know each other?" Gonzo asks, his eyes flicking between where Robby is still holding Ainsley's hand.

"We go way back," Ty says.

"We used to date," Robby states.

Gonzo chokes. "All three of you?"

Brandon laughs, a hearty sound that echoes throughout the dressing room. "Nah. Just the two of them. I came along after they broke up."

"Cool. Nice to meet you, have you join the crew. The extended family is all super supportive."

There are footsteps behind us, and I turn in the direction of the sound. "We should probably get to our seats."

"Hey, Cap!" Gonzo says. "Come meet Amelia's family."

My gaze locks on McKittrick's, the hard set of his jaw. And then, against my will, my eyes sweep over his form. He's only wearing his base layer on the bottom, his chest bare. His body is every bit as cut up close as I imagined it would be from far away.

I haven't had the chance to work on him since that first day, and he was fully clothed at the time. I was focused on his knee, not on the rest of him.

And the rest of him is potent.

"Guests aren't allowed in the dressing room," McKittrick says tightly.

"Oh. We'll get out of the way," Brandon says. He runs a hand over Ainsley's back, shifting his weight as she makes a soft noise.

"I invited them," Robby says. "We're on our way back to the equipment cave."

McKittrick grunts.

"Sorry to intrude," my brother says. "I'm Tyler, and this is my husband, Brandon."

The hockey player nods, guarded. "Jason McKittrick."

Brandon cocks his head. "Haven't I seen you before?"

"I'm your neighbor," McKittrick says. "My living room window faces yours."

Tyler frowns. "So, you're the asshole who doesn't close his blinds."

I choke. Does he know about the private shows?

No. He can't. There's no way he knows.

"You guys don't close your curtains, either," McKittrick says lightly.

MacGregor and Logan shuffle past us. The redhead stops suddenly, and Logan slams into his back.

"What the fuck, man," Logan mutters.

"You're Brandon Walker," MacGregor says.

Guarded, my brother-in-law nods. "Yeah." Just because he's in a pro hockey dressing room doesn't mean people can't get weird.

"Shit, man," he says. "Aidan MacGregor. I'm a huge fan."

"Yeah?" Brandon grins, offering his hand.

"You're always the first pick on my fantasy team," MacGregor says. "You and Austin Anderson are, like, the dream team."

Logan groans. "He's not going to shut up about this for a month."

Brandon flushes, a pleased smile on his face. "Sorry, not sorry."

"Nah, man, it's cool," Logan says. "We all need our hobbies."

"I played ball through high school. Gave it up to get serious about hockey, but fuck, sometimes I miss it."

"Well, if you ever want to toss a ball around, hit me up," Brandon says.

MacGregor gapes at him. "I think I love you."

"He's married," Tyler says, with a smirk.

The hockey player shrugs. "Didn't say I was going to propose."

McKittrick clears his throat. "We need to get ready for our game."

"Yes. Right. The game." MacGregor nods. "You guys heading to the bar after?"

"Nah. We have to get the little one home," Brandon says. "We'll stay for the game, but taking an infant to a bar probably won't win us any parenting points."

"Good call," Logan says. He gives us a broad smile. "Nice meeting you guys. Hailey's up in the family suite, if you want to join her."

That's MacGregor's sister. I met her once. She's nice, if a bit quiet.

"Thanks, man," Ty says. "Nice to meet you all."

Robby leads us down the hallway to the equipment cave, where he spends most of his time sharpening skates, mending jerseys, and getting all the equipment ready.

Sinclair rummages through one of the cabinets, coming up with a roll of tape.

"Hey. Is it bring your family to work day?" He grins at us, his hockey smile missing two teeth courtesy of a high stick to the face last week.

"Something like that," I mutter. "You're good and loose?" I worked on his hamstring a few hours ago.

He nods. "Feeling great. Thanks for the assist."

"Any time. You know where to find me."

He shuffles off. My work day is technically over, since I'm not on shift for the game. Zac already left, and Graham and Derek will handle everything. It feels weird to just go home when the guys are playing, though. I'm just as much part of the team as any other staff member.

After a few more minutes chatting with Robby, I lead my brothers through the tunnels to the stands. My comp tickets are in the nosebleeds, but I don't think the guys care. They're more focused on getting out of the house and drinking beer than on the game itself.

With a Grizzlies ball cap pulled low, nobody else recognizes Brandon, and we enjoy the game from the uncomfortable stadium seats with our overpriced beer and snacks. Ainsley sleeps through most of the game, her little ears protected by giant muffs. When she wakes up, Tyler and Brandon take turns walking her around the upper concourse, turning down my repeated offers to take a shift.

The guys look good on the ice. They're up two points over Tampa, and after losing their last two games, the team is hungry for redemption. MacGregor and Larsson have each scored goals. McKittrick landed five shots on goal by himself. He wants a goal—he wants it *bad*.

They're in the offensive zone when MacGregor wins the face-off. He kicks the puck back to Logan, who pressures the Tampa forwards, dekes past a defenseman, and shoots.

The goalie blocks the shot—pad save.

But the rebound—it goes right to McKittrick's stick. He may be one of the oldest players in the league, but his one-timer is still brutal.

And with a flick of his wrist, he buries the puck in the back of the net. The lamp lights red, and the goal horn sounds.

The guys crowd McKittrick in a circle for celebratory hugs, and then he leads the charge down the line of teammates for fist bumps.

My smile stretches from ear to ear. I wish I could be on the ice with them, watching from my safe space in the tunnel, but it's almost sweeter to watch from the stands. I get to appreciate it with thousands of fans.

And when the night's over and I'm alone in my room, the lights turned down low, I wait for McKittrick to get back to his place. He stops short when he sees me waiting for him.

He cocks his head, the lights behind him concealing his features.

But I know him well enough to understand he wants this.

I drop my robe.

He doesn't look away.

The man got a goal tonight, bringing home the W for the team. The least thing I can do is give him another show.

Although really… I think I'm the one winning here.

twelve

. . .

Jason

THE BAGEL SHOP IS CROWDED, but given that it's a Sunday morning, I wouldn't expect anything less. There's a reason so many people come here; the bagels are that amazing.

I'm feeling good after our win last night—and my private show after. My knee doesn't even hurt. I haven't felt this good in a long time, at least since Harper served me with the divorce papers. I'm finally feeling like myself again.

Shuffling into line, I notice the dark-haired beauty in front of me, and my dick instantly reacts. I adjust my stance and clear my throat, but it does nothing to quench the heat simmering just beneath my skin.

I want her. I can't have her, and I fucking want her anyway.

The line shuffles forward, and we all take a step.

Amelia is wearing jeans and a long-sleeved top, her hair pulled back from her face with a pink silk scrunchie. I wonder if it's the same one she wore that night we slept together.

Ahem. Shared a bed. *Her* bed.

I still don't know how that happened. She didn't say

anything the next day, so I didn't either. I must have been pretty messed up for her to take me back to her room.

But nothing happened. Deep in my heart, I *know* nothing inappropriate happened between us. Even if I wanted it to, I was in no shape to act on my feelings. Fuck, I probably couldn't have even gotten it up with the amount of whiskey I had.

She steps up to the counter, placing an order for two dozen bagels, and then moves off to the side while they pack it up.

The clerk waves me forward, and I order my usual pumpernickel, tomato, and lox sandwich. It's my Sunday morning treat. Also, we have the day off—I can deviate from the diet plan just a smidge.

As I move to the counter to pay, I notice Amelia do a double take from the corner of my eye. I tap my card and join her at the side of the counter, waiting for my order.

"Good morning," I say, slipping my wallet back into my pocket.

"Morning."

Do I bring up last night's show?

"Good game last night," she finally says. "Congrats on the goal."

"Thanks." Pride puffs up my chest. It was a dirty goal, but they don't all have to be pretty as long as they're effective.

And it was. It brought the tally to three and one, and we took home the win.

"So, your brothers…"

Her shoulders tense. "Yeah? What about them?"

"I didn't realize he was a ball player."

"Yep." Her voice is tight. "He's okay."

I choke out a laugh. "He was the league MVP twice in three years. He's won four Golden Glove awards. *And* he's not even thirty yet!"

"Eh." She shrugs.

Gaping, I turn to face her, and notice the laughter dancing in her eyes.

"For real, I'm incredibly proud of him," Amelia says. "He worked his ass off to get to where he is. He's one of my heroes."

"MacGregor's, too." The dude is obsessed with baseball.

She chuckles. "Yeah, I could tell. What about you? You into baseball?"

I shrug. "I mean, I support all Boston sports. But unless it's a specific matchup, I'm not usually watching. Was kind of busy last summer."

"Right. With the divorce and all."

Wincing, I say, "You heard about that?"

"I'm sorry." She cocks her head. "Isn't that what you're supposed to say?"

"Eh. I'm not sorry. It needed to end. We had nothing to say to each other anymore."

"Still. It must be difficult."

"It's over." The finality in my tone makes her blink, and I clear my throat. "I don't think about her anymore. We aren't in contact. I'm moving on."

She already has. We sold the house, and Harper moved in with her new guy before the ink on the divorce decree dried.

"Amelia!" The shop clerk holds out two heavy bags and another calls out, "Jason!"

"Need help carrying that?" I ask as I take my tiny little sandwich bag.

Her eyes flash. "Why? Because I'm a woman and obviously—"

"Because those bags are full, and the straps don't look strong enough to support their weight," I snap back.

She blinks.

"Besides, we're basically going to the same place."

Our apartments are three blocks away.

"Fine. If you insist." Scowling, she hands over one bag, keeping the other for herself.

"Give me both. I can handle it."

She grumbles under her breath, but she does as I ask. Such a brat. We trade until she's holding my little bag, and I'm carrying her two bulging bags.

"After you."

We walk in silence for a block and a half before she turns to me.

"Thanks," Amelia says, so quietly I almost think I imagined it.

"Any time." I adjust the weight of the bagels in my grasp. "What are you doing with so many bagels? Do you freeze them?"

"We're having bagel brunch." She pauses. "Do you… would you like to join us?"

"Sure." It's not like I have anything better to do with my Sunday.

And secretly, I'm dying to get to know her, to find out what makes her tick.

Acting on this attraction is a bad idea, but I can fantasize in the privacy of my head all I want. Nobody has to know.

A doorman opens the front door, and Amelia scans a fob at the turnstile, granting us access to the elevator bank. She punches the button for the nineteenth floor.

"You totally don't have to stay, if you don't want to," she says as the elevator hurtles upward. "I don't want to pressure you into it."

"You're not." My chuckle sounds forced. "Trust me, if I didn't want to stay, I'd have no problem heading home."

"Well, it's so far away." I think there's a hint of a smile, if I squint.

"Better than sitting in my place and watching you guys have a party without me," I point out.

She lets out a little giggle, the sound bringing a smile to my face.

"Come on. Don't say I didn't warn you."

We exit on her floor, and she leads me down the hallway to her front door. There's a mat out front that reads "Welcome-ish: Depends on who you are and how long you're staying."

Instantly, I know this isn't her decoration, but she whole-heartedly agrees with it. If I had to wager a guess, it was Tyler's find, but Brandon's the one who displayed it out in the hall rather than inside the front door.

"Honey, I'm home," Amelia calls as she opens the front door. "Please be wearing clothes."

"Oh, fuck off," Brandon says, striding down the hallway to meet us. His hair is rumpled, his shirt buttons off-skew. "We finished up ten minutes ago."

She makes a face. "I already have to hear you having sex every night. You don't need to give me a play-by-play, too."

He slings an arm over her shoulder. "Well, sweetie, when two people love each other very much—"

She elbows him in the gut, and he coughs.

"I brought McKittrick," she says, hooking a thumb over her shoulder. "Come on, you can set the bagels in the kitchen."

Tyler is wearing a black apron over a collared shirt, slicing tomatoes. "You took forever," he complains.

"The shop was busy. Next time, you can go get them your-self," she snaps.

"Nah. Much rather send you." He smirks. "She roped you into helping?"

"Something like that," I mutter. "Good to see you again."

"I invited him to stay," she adds.

"Glad to have you." Brandon claps me on the back, and then takes one bag from my arms. "The more, the merrier."

"Anything I can do to help?" I offer.

"Nah. Just chill for a bit. Want a coffee? Or a beer?"

"Coffee would be great." I drop the other bag on the counter.

Amelia bustles through the small kitchen to the coffeemaker, pulling down a mug from the cupboard and popping a pod into the machine.

"So, you do this often? Bagel brunch?"

"In the off-season, as much as we can," Brandon says. "Gotta enjoy the downtime while it lasts."

"I feel that." Although baseball gets more time off than hockey does, it always feels like the weeks slip by.

Tyler arranges the tomatoes on a platter, layering it with the red onion and cucumber already sliced. It's only then that I look over at the table. It's set for ten.

"I don't want to impose."

"You're not," Amelia says, bringing me a hot pink mug. The side says "Bad Bitch."

If she thinks she's embarrassing me by giving me this one, she isn't. I'm definitely a Bad Bitch.

"I added cream, no sugar," she adds.

I blink. She knows my coffee order. Opening my mouth, she cuts me off.

"Shut up," she snaps.

"Shutting up," I repeat obediently, and her eyes flash.

In short order, we're banished from the kitchen, and we retreat to the sofa while Tyler finishes preparing everything.

"He's kind of a perfectionist," Brandon says, fondness softening his face. "He doesn't get to cook nearly as much as he used to."

"Oh?"

"Ty's a chef," Amelia adds.

"He gave up the restaurant gig when we moved to Boston," his husband adds. "He has a meal delivery business, preparing food for guys on the team." He cocks his head. "I think some of the Grizzlies are on his service, too, come to think of it."

"If they aren't yet, they will be soon," Ty calls from the kitchen. "I'm just biding my time."

"Do you work with a dietitian?" I ask.

Brandon nods. "He has someone on staff, but if you have a team nutritionist you receive orders from, he's happy to work with them. His clientele is almost exclusively athletes."

"That's really neat. I hate cooking, and to be honest, it's getting more and more difficult to stay on the diet plan," I admit. Harper did most of my meal preparation. She was a much better cook than me.

"Well, if you want to be added to the roster, take Ty's card," Brandon says. "He'll whip something up for you."

"You're my best salesman," the chef says from the other room. "Love you."

"Love you more," the baseball player sings back.

There's a knock at the door, and Amelia stands to greet the guests. To my surprise, it's Larsson and his fiancée, Vanessa.

"Thank you for inviting us," the Swede says in his crisp accent. His hand clenches Vanessa's tightly, his face strained. He's not one for socializing. It's a marker of how much he loves her that he's able to set aside his personal discomfort for her benefit.

"I'm so glad you made it." Amelia ushers them in. "Can I get you anything to drink?"

Larsson shakes his head, and then catches sight of me in the room. His eyes widen.

"Come in, come in." She goes to close the door when something makes her pause.

But it's only Andrews, Joaquin, and Patrice, the other staffers she hangs out with. Now I definitely feel like the odd man out.

"I brought booze," Andrews says, holding up a bottle of champagne and another of vodka.

"Now the party's started," Brandon says, with a grin. "Bloody Marys?"

"Fuck, yes." He cocks his head when he clocks me in the room. "Hey, McKittrick. You're joining us for brunch?"

"Yeah. That okay?"

"We'll kick you out when we're done with you," Tyler says with a laugh from the kitchen. He brings a platter laden with bagels to the table. "Come, let's eat."

thirteen

. . .

Amelia

I'M the last to sit down, so of course, the only empty seat is beside McKittrick.

Jason.

If he's thrown by our coworkers being here, he doesn't show it.

"Wow," he mutters. "He really went all out."

The table is filled with bagels and a relish tray, plus a platter of deviled eggs, a winter vegetable salad, tuna salad, and a frittata. And that doesn't include the pitcher of Bloody Marys and another jug of orange juice for mimosas.

"We used to do this all the time in Austin," Tyler says. "Brando's teammates aren't into brunch, they prefer steakhouses. And while I can cook a mean Tomahawk, it's not my favorite."

"Well, I'm glad you invited us," Vanessa says. "I love those meals you drop off. You're supremely talented."

He grins. "I'll get the entire roster soon enough."

"If you need help with the logistics of it all, let me know. That's my department."

"You got it."

I knew connecting Ty with the hockey team was a good

move. He only works part-time right now, easing back into the swing of things after his paternity leave. But he could easily leave everything to his chefs and just handle the business side of things. Then again, he started the business because he missed cooking, so who's to say he can't find someone to run the numbers while he does the chef-y work?

I've only been with the team for two months, but already, Vanessa, Patrice, Joaquin, Robby, and I are forming a tight little group. We sit together on the plane, we go for meals together, and most of our free time is spent together. When you travel as much as we do, it's nice to have a core group of friends amongst the coworkers. I didn't really have that in Colorado.

To my surprise, it isn't weird having two players with us. Maybe because one of them is Sven, who doesn't talk much on a good day, and McKittrick is the middleman between the staff and players.

The man drinks his coffee in the hot pink mug, seemingly content to sit there amongst the hubbub of the group. Joaquin and Tyler get along fabulously, just like I hoped they would, and Patrice and Brandon are talking about the signings the Bulldogs made in the off-season.

Robby's eyes are misty, and I give him a little kick under the table.

"You okay?" I mouth.

He nods, swallowing thickly. "I'm just so happy."

"Why wouldn't you be happy?" Patrice asks.

"When I came out… I knew it wouldn't be great, but I wasn't prepared for how rough it really got," Robby says. "I'm not perfect, not in the slightest, and two of the people I hurt the most are sitting here at this table, like nothing is wrong, and I just—I'm so fucking happy."

"Oh, Rob," Tyler sighs. "That's water under the bridge."

"We're good now," Vanessa adds. "Really."

Robby shakes his head. "I'm so fucking grateful we got to this point. And that we can hang out and it's not weird."

"It's a little weird," Joaquin cuts in.

Robby flips him off. "I'm finally living the life I wanted to live. My authentic truth. And as much as I regret that it took so long to get here, now that I'm here, I don't want to give it up."

"And you don't have to," Brandon says firmly. "We're here to support you. All of us are."

"Yeah, man," McKittrick adds in. "This team is a family. We've got each other's backs, no matter what."

My eyes well up with tears at their unconditional acceptance. It's what he should have gotten when he told his parents; it's what Brandon should have had with his family; it's what Ty should have received from our dad.

Family is more than flesh and blood; it's the people we choose to keep in our lives, the people who lift us up rather than drag us down.

The baby monitor squeals as Ainsley squawks in the other room.

"I've got her," I tell my brothers when they both start to rise. "It's my turn."

"Thanks, Meels," Ty says, and then shoves a giant piece of bagel into his mouth.

Slipping from the table, I head to the nursery, the baby's cries increasing in volume as she wakes up. I lift her from the crib, her entire body scrunched, and snuggle her, inhaling her fresh scent for a second before she gets angry.

After a quick diaper change, I pad down the hallway to the main room, the now-quiet baby content in my arms.

"How's my perfect girl?" Ty asks from the kitchen, where he's preparing a bottle.

"I'm well, thank you," I retort.

To my surprise, Sven laughs. It's the most emotion he's shown today.

"Don't be a smart ass," my brother teases, handing me the bottle. "Want me to handle it?"

"I've got it. We need some girl time."

Settling back at the table, I adjust Ainsley into a better position, and then slip the bottle between her puckering lips.

McKittrick's stare is like a brand. My skin prickles with goosebumps at the intensity of his gaze. His body radiates heat, warmth rolling off him in waves.

I don't want kids of my own, but I can't deny it's intimate when his eyes are on me while I feed the baby I birthed. Even though Ainsley isn't my child, even though there's nothing between me and McKittrick... I still feel it. It's palpable, the air so thick with tension I can hardly breathe for fear it will crush me.

"She's beautiful," Patrice says, drawing my attention away from the man beside me. "You did a good job."

"It's all Brando's genes," I deflect.

"Still. You did the hard work," my brother-in-law says. "Now give me my baby."

He approaches and I slide her into his arms, sending the bottle with him. Bringing her close, he snuggles her and kisses her forehead. She doesn't like the interruption from her meal, making a mewl of protest before he situates the bottle again and she settles back in.

Joaquin, Robby, and Patrice coo over the baby, but McKittrick's attention is on me. His eyes are hazy as he stares at me, clearly lost in thought.

I wonder what he's thinking about. I don't think he had kids with his ex-wife. Is he wishing he did?

"You're good with her," Vanessa says, almost wistfully. "How did you learn?"

"Trial and error." Laughing, I add, "and error, and error, and error."

Sven slides his arm around her shoulders, and she leans

into him. "I hope I'm as good with our baby," she says, and her fiancé kisses her temple.

Beside me, McKittrick freezes. "You're having a baby?" he repeats slowly, his eyes wide.

Sven nods. "Due in March."

And then the hockey captain grins, his entire body relaxing. "Congratulations, Van, Larsson. You'll be excellent parents."

Larsson nods. "We have much to learn." He looks terrified.

"It gets easier," Brandon tells him. "Certain things get more difficult, but learning as you go is part of the job."

"I like to know. I like to study." The Swede shakes his head. "I do not like to *go with the flow.*"

Vanessa laughs. "We know, babe." She pats his leg. "But we have some time before we need to worry about that. At least five more months."

McKittrick runs his hand through his hair, the chocolate brown strands lifting to show the grey sprinkled in beneath them. "A baby. You know the team is will flip."

A few of the players already have kids, but none of them are in relationships with staff members.

"We're not making a big announcement," Vanessa says. "I've told Jacky and Coach, plus these guys. Everyone who needs to know does."

"Thank you for including me in that." McKittrick's hand is on his chest, and his eyes are misty. "I appreciate you telling me."

"You're our captain," Larsson says, as if that's all there is to it.

And maybe for him, that's all it is.

I'm the first to admit I don't know McKittrick well. Our first few interactions didn't lend themselves to a positive working relationship. And then when he got wasted…

He's a complicated man, going through a tumultuous time

in his life. The ending of his marriage, the sunset of his career... Either one would be a lot to deal with, and to do it simultaneously, he must be stronger than anyone knows.

I wonder if he ever lets himself fall apart. Who picks up the pieces? Does he hold it all inside, or does he confide in anyone?

For some reason, I have this insane urge to be there for him. To support him. To give him a shoulder to lean on. Even the strongest people need a break sometimes. An outlet for all the chaos simmering beneath the surface.

Maybe my shows muddy the waters. All I know is that he hasn't looked away, not once. He's just as hungry for them as I am.

He needs them as much as me.

fourteen

. . .

Amelia

I'M SENDING Sinclair on his way when McKittrick approaches the PT bay.

"You okay?" I ask, even though he's favoring his left leg.

"I could use a look at my knee," the captain says, nodding at Sinclair. "You have time?"

Oh, good, so he's not avoiding me outright. I was afraid that would happen.

"I have half an hour until my next session." Stepping back, I usher him into the small, windowless room I've claimed as my own.

Graham is on his lunch break, and Zac is with Derek going over a treatment plan with Trevor, so we have the med suite to ourselves.

McKittrick is wearing athletic shorts and a performance t-shirt with the Grizzlies logo on the chest. His hair is damp, most likely fresh out of the shower, his woodsy scent amplified when he brushes past me to the table.

I do a visual examination first. Everything looks to be in order—no bruising, bleeding, or swelling. Snapping on a fresh pair of gloves, I palpate his knee, watching his face for any indication of pain or tenderness.

"You need to stop." His voice is hoarse, his entire body a solid line of tension.

"What's hurting?" Removing my hand from his leg, I take a step back, assessing. I've barely touched him. I wasn't overly aggressive…

He pauses.

"Is it the—"

"I need you to stop," he says again, more harshly. His breathing is coming faster now, his massive chest rising and falling with each stuttered breath.

"Mc—"

And that's when I see it. The bulge in his shorts has grown significantly, tenting the stretchy mesh fabric.

Keeping my face neutral, I tell him, "It's totally natural. You don't need to be embarrassed. It's a physical reaction."

"Stop talking." His face flames and he scrunches his eyes, like that will make it go away.

"But—"

"Amelia," he says, his voice rough like sandpaper. Heat coils deep in my belly at the sound, and I clench my thighs together. "I'm ten seconds away from throwing you down on this table, so if you don't shut the hell up right fucking now—"

"You'll do what?"

His eyes open, and he turns to look at me, his green eyes nearly eclipsed by his pupils. "We can't."

"Why not?" I cross my arms over my chest, hiding the way my nipples have beaded into tight buds.

"It's inappropriate," he grunts, scrubbing a hand over his face.

I pull off my gloves, and then set my hand on his thigh again. Higher. My fingertips run along the hem of his shorts, the rasp of his body hair on my skin doing dangerous things to my heart rate.

"Do you know what you're doing, little girl?" His eyes lock on mine, daring me to go further.

I've never backed down from a challenge.

Sliding my hands over his shorts, I tease my way to his hip, tiptoeing my way over the socket. The bulge twitches, and my mouth waters. I wonder what he looks like up close. I want to taste him, to lick him from root to tip. My pussy clenches around emptiness, leaving me wanting.

"Amelia…"

When I cup his erection, it throbs in my grip, his pulse fluttering in his neck. I squeeze gently, the hard, thick length so wonderfully reactive.

He surges upright. Before I can so much as blink, McKittrick's hand is on my throat, pulling me toward him. His lips descend on mine, licking into my mouth, like he's as desperate for this as me. With his grip on my throat, he can feel every breath I take, the rapid-fire thundering of my pulse.

His hand lands on my hip, pulling me into the V of his legs, and then slips around to my ass, squeezing the rounded flesh. I set mine on his thighs, pushing them apart, and then slide my hand back to his erection, palming the thick length. He fills my fist so beautifully.

McKittrick groans into the kiss, his tongue stroking mine.

"This is a bad idea," he breathes.

"So stop," I counter.

His dark chuckle vibrates against my lips. "Take off your pants."

Rearing back, I search his eyes. I must have misheard him.

"Take off your fucking pants, Amelia," he says roughly, his hand resting on the column of my throat.

But he doesn't exert any pressure.

It's entirely up to me. I could stop this at any time. But I don't *want* to stop it. We've been heading for this ever since that very first time. It's always been inevitable.

And I can't fucking wait another second.

I take a step back, and he releases me. Heaving in a breath, my fingers fumble with the button on my jeans. His eyes pin me to the spot.

Slowly, I work the denim over my hips. He nods at me, his eyes dark, and I step out of the jeans, dropping them on the counter behind me.

"Panties, too," he growls.

"Or what?" I arch an eyebrow.

"Little girl…"

I cross my arms over my chest. "I'm not a *little girl*. I'm a grown ass woman."

"You're ten years younger than me."

"So? If you want to find someone young and naïve to play with, go ahead. But it won't be me."

Quick as lightning, his fingers hook in the front of my panties, pulling the elastic band down to expose the top of my mound. His wrist twists, and then he's sliding three fingers between my legs, gliding through the wetness there.

"You sure about that?"

I widen my stance to give him more access. "If you want to play, it'll be with me, not some innocent little virgin who—"

My words cut off when he thrusts two fingers inside me. My walls flutter around the intrusion, so fucking full.

"You're right," he growls. "You're not innocent, not in the slightest. Not with the shows you give me."

Victorious, I grin. "You like them?"

His fingers withdraw, and then fuck into me a few times, each thrust leaving me wanting more.

"Fucking hate them," he says, slamming his mouth over mine. His kiss is ruthless, wrenching the breath from my lungs.

He hates them? But he watches every one.

"Hate you being so fucking far away," he murmurs against my lips. "Hate not touching you, tasting you." He bites my lip, soothing the sting away with his tongue. "Hate not hearing you. Having you."

"You have me now." I gasp as his thumb rubs my clit.

My eyes roll back in my head from the sensory overload. My hand is loosely wrapped around his cock, the fabric in my way. I move to his waistband, but his hand lands on mine, guiding me away.

"Don't distract me." It's not a request, it's an order, and my cunt throbs around his fingers. I shouldn't love being bossed around as much as I do.

Hands clenching to his thighs, I can do little more than hold on while he touches me, rough and frantic, like he's even halfway as worked up as I am. As if he needs this as much as I do.

He knows exactly what to do to drive me crazy and crazier. My skin is tight, like I'm about to burst out of it, and just when I think I can't take it anymore, I shatter.

I splinter apart, thousands of tiny shards breaking into a million more. The air is punched from my lungs as pleasure overtakes me, my body helpless to the sensations wreaking havoc on my system.

My knees buckle, and I pitch forward, McKittrick's hand leaving my throat to move to my hip, stabilizing me. I collapse against him, stealing some of his steadiness. Slowly, he pulls his fingers out from where they're buried deep within me, and I watch as he brings them to his mouth, licking them clean.

I whimper. I fucking *whimper*, like I'm the heroine in a regency romance novel.

The smirk he gives me is so fucking devilish. He knows he's a fucking rake.

McKittrick is a tightly coiled ball of tension, and even though I came, he hasn't. I've barely even touched him.

Once I'm certain I can stand on my own two feet again, I

step away, rummaging through the cabinets behind me. He lets out a soft groan of protest. But I'm not ignoring him.

Coming up with the massage oil, I return to him.

"Take off your pants," I order. It's my turn now.

Breathing hard, he slips off the table, the thick length of his erection brushing against my hip. We're standing toe-to-toe, and although he's a whole foot taller than me, I don't feel unsafe. I don't feel pressured. Deep in my soul, I know he'd never make me do anything I wasn't comfortable with.

He drops his pants.

My mouth waters as I take him in. Thick and long, with a dark mushroom head, the tip leaking pre-cum. I reach for him, desperate to touch him, when I remember the massage oil in my hand.

Squeezing the oil into my palms, I rub them together to warm it before I wrap my fist around his erection. McKittrick blows out a breath, his eyes locked on where my hand circles around his length. I give him a firm stroke, and then a second. He reaches for me, ducking his head to kiss me again.

His tongue plunges into my mouth, tasting me, devouring me. He bites at my lips and soothes the sting, brutally attentive.

In my hand, his cock is hard as stone, smooth steel encased in velvet. A drop of pre-cum beads at the tip, and I smooth it along his shaft, the stickiness mixing with the oil to ease my strokes.

His hand closes around mine, pulling it away.

"What's wrong?" I ask, already missing the feel of him as his cock bobs between us.

"Turn around and bend over," McKittrick says roughly.

Anticipation swirls in my belly. "I don't have any condoms."

"We don't need condoms."

Alarm bells go off in my brain, and I push on his chest. It's hard as stone, and he doesn't move an inch.

"What do you mean? If you're going to fuck me—"

"I'm not going to fuck you." A muscle clenches in his jaw. "Turn around and bend over."

I meet his eyes. It's true that I've enjoyed every moment of this so far. I trust him. If I didn't, I wouldn't let him put his hands on me in the first place.

So, I turn around. Bend over.

He clicks the cap of the massage oil, and then I hear the sound of skin-on-skin, and then his body is behind mine. The head of his cock brushes against my ass, and I tense.

But then he shifts, his hand maneuvering against my ass, and he guides his cock between my legs.

I squeeze my thighs together, giving him a tight channel to fuck into. His groan reverberates through him and into me, rattling my bones.

His hands land on my hips, his grip tight, and he blankets my body with his, the heat between us turning the room into an inferno. His mouth lands on my neck, licking and sucking at the skin.

With the remaining air in my lungs, I gasp out, "No marks."

Scraping his teeth against the tendon in my neck, he growls but backs off. His hips buck against my ass while he fucks my thighs, the thick, sticky length of him so fucking close to my pussy.

But he doesn't fuck me, doesn't try to enter me.

His thrusts grow more erratic, his breathing harsh and ragged in my ear. I arch my back, pressing my ass against him, and his entire body tenses as he lets out a long, loud groan.

Between my legs, his cock pulses, his cum landing on my skin and on the exam table. His body shakes behind me, finally going still.

The only sound in the room the ragged breaths sawing out of our lungs. Both of us are struggling to breathe, and I don't know about him, but my heart races like I just ran a fucking marathon.

Or a marathon fucking.

McKittrick clears his throat, and then steps back. I feel the loss of him immediately, and I'm suddenly hit with the awareness that his cum is between my thighs while I'm at *work.*

We did this in my office. At work. Where anyone could walk in and see us. Hear us.

Fuck.

He crosses the small room and grabs a few paper towels, wetting them at the sink, and then brings them to me to clean myself up. He does the same, and then pulls his shorts back on and runs his hand through his hair.

"Uh..."

I shake my head. "Just go."

He clears his throat. "My, uh, knee..."

"Right." With a sigh, I cross the room to the sink, washing my hands, and then wipe down the table. "Hop back up."

A pleased smirk on his lips, McKittrick lays himself out on my table, and I focus on the task at hand, testing his mobility and then assigning him specific exercises as homework.

I can't fool around with the hockey team captain. I can't fuck around at work. He's practically untouchable; they'd get rid of me in an instant.

It doesn't matter that our brief *interlude* was the highlight of my year. It can't happen again.

fifteen

. . .

Jason

THEY TELL you in divorce circles is that you'll eventually, get back on the dating horse, and when you do, you'll experience the cycle of grief all over again. I didn't believe them. I was stronger than that.

But it's been three days since Amelia wrecked my world, and I still don't know how I feel about it.

Harper was supposed to be my forever, and even though she's happier without me, and I'm doing fine on my own without her… A part of me thought I would never be able to move on again. That I'd never experience *new* again.

I don't miss her. I grieved for our relationship. I truly thought I'd moved on.

But fooling around with Amelia made one thing clear: I never thought I'd be happy with another person again. It was a self-limiting belief. I didn't trust myself.

As much as I want another chance with Amelia, it's not a good idea. Not while she works for the team. And especially not with me looking into her bedroom window every night.

Trudging through my apartment, I do my best not to look to my left as I turn on the coffeemaker and set a bagel to toast. I don't look over when I wash the dishes I didn't take care of last night. And I force my eyes not to rise as I eat my breakfast.

Fuck it. I look over.

And then my chest fucking pangs, like I'm a heartbroken teenager.

Amelia paces the living room of her apartment, holding baby Ainsley in the air and bouncing her. Tyler lounges on the couch behind her, holding a cup of coffee to his lips, and as I watch, Brandon crosses the space to sit beside his husband, wrapping his arm around Tyler's shoulders.

She's happy. They all are.

Our encounter in the PT bay was hot as hell, but it can't happen again. It's a bad idea. Doesn't keep me from wanting it, though.

Being with Amelia was like breathing fresh air, like finding a heated building in the middle of a blizzard. I didn't realize how frozen I was until I thawed. *She* helped me thaw.

And now… where does that leave us?

If she didn't work for the team, I'd still want to pursue. Our being in close proximity, working together, and traveling together is a big part of our electric connection. If we weren't confined to tight spaces over and over again, I don't know if we'd combust, or if it would be a long, drawn-out slow burn.

One thing's for certain: there would definitely be fireworks.

And I certainly can't ask her to leave her job so we can be together. Do I even want us to be together? Can't it just be a one-and-done, and we go our separate ways now that we both got what we wanted?

No. There's a fire simmering in my veins, burning me up from the inside out. I want another round with her. I want ten more. A hundred more. I don't know if I'll ever get enough of her.

There's a knock on my door, and I flinch at the sound. It's

ten o'clock on our day off. Who the fuck is seeking me out now?

Reluctantly, I open the door, glaring at the interloper daring to interrupt me.

Ryan Logan, the team's best defenseman, flinches. "Fuck. This is a bad idea."

I blow out a breath. "Did you ask her out?"

"No." He sighs. "I don't know how much longer I can keep doing this."

"Come on in."

Holding the door open, I usher him in, and then head over to the sofa. The TV is on ESPN, as usual, but the volume is muted. I fucking hate the talking heads. All they do is rip us apart.

Thank goodness our team's station isn't bad. Jared Aviyente, the team's sportscaster, does a decent job analyzing our plays without making us feel like dog shit for messing up.

Because we all mess up sometimes. We're human.

"What happened?" I ask Logan, who's slumped on my couch.

"I'm in love with her."

His feelings for his best friend's little sister were always clear as day. Everyone knows—except MacGregor. The idiot's rather oblivious.

"No, shit."

His head snaps up, and he glares at me. "Fuck off."

"Hey, you're the one on my sofa. What happened *now*?"

He sighs. "Our high school reunion is coming up in a few months. I got a call from the organizing committee. They want me to come, and will work with our schedule to make sure I'm available."

"And you want to ask her to go with you?"

"I don't want to show up to the reunion alone like a loser. Like I'm still a twenty-eight year old vir—" He clamps his lips together. "I want to go with Hailey. I want to *be with* Hailey. And she has no interest in me."

"I'm not so sure about that."

MacGregor's sister hangs out with the team. She comes to almost all of our home games, and volunteers with the Grizzlies Foundation. Decent person. Hell, she's her brother's date to our formal functions.

But it's not a weird thing. They lost their parents young, and she's disabled and depends on him for a lot of things.

Logan slots into their dynamic seamlessly. He grew up with the MacGregor siblings. I don't know all the details, but everyone knows they're a tightly knit trio.

… which might be part of the problem, come to think about it.

"Have you talked to MacGregor? Asked for his blessing?"

Logan flinches. "I shouldn't have to *ask his permission*. She's a grown ass adult."

"Yeah, but he's your best friend." I shake my head. "And it's not asking for his permission, it's his approval. Because if he doesn't want you to date his sister…"

"I don't care what he thinks," Logan says. "I love her."

Hiding my wince, I clear my throat. "I know you do. But my job as your captain is to tell you that it can't happen."

His face falls.

"Not without MacGregor's blessing. You two are best friends. He's your teammate. We can't have discord in the locker room." I blow out a breath. "For what it's worth, I think you and Hailey would be good together. But if it comes down to it, who are you going to pick—her, or your teammate?"

"Her," he says without hesitation.

"And see, that's why, as your captain, I have to tell you it's a bad idea."

I don't want to. It isn't my place to keep him from the woman he loves. But at the end of the day, my role is to guide this team, and I can't do that effectively if the players aren't focused on the goal.

"Until you get to the point of putting a ring on her finger, you have to focus on your career first," I tell him. "Right now, she's a wish you want to come true. It's not reality. And the reality is, you have to work with him all day, every day. Can you really look him in the eye on the ice and then go behind his back with his little sister?"

Logan sighs, sinking into the couch. "No. I can't."

"I'm not saying it can never happen. But maybe not for this reunion."

"You know we grew up together? I wanted to ask her to prom." He shakes his head. "Chickened out. I didn't have the courage to do it. And I've kicked myself for the last ten years. I thought when I signed here that we might be able to start something, but..."

"But MacGregor is in the way," I finish.

"Yeah. And he's my best friend. I love him like a brother. I wouldn't trade our relationship for the world..." He scrubs a hand over his face. "But I can see a future with Hailey. An honest future. And she's not interested in that life, not with me." Letting out a sigh, he shakes his head. "I just don't know how to move on from that. I've loved her since we were fifteen. Ever since I knew how to want a girl, it's always been her. It's *only* been her."

"Have you tried dating someone else?"

"Not interested." Logan pauses, biting his lip like he has something else to say, but isn't ready yet.

"I'm here for you, man. Anything you say to me is private."

"I'm demisexual," the defenseman says. "I only experience attraction to someone I know well. And I can't very well ask someone out and say, hey, I'm not attracted to you, and I might never be, but sure, let's waste your time until we figure out if we clicks. Because *that's* not a shit ton of pressure to put on someone else."

Reaching over, I set my hand on his shoulder. "Is this the first time you came out to someone?"

He gives me a rueful grin. "Second time. The first... it didn't go so well."

"Well, fuck, man. I appreciate you sharing with me."

"You're my captain." Logan shrugs. "It's not just lust with me and Hailey. I have actual feelings for her. I can picture spending the rest of my life with her."

"Because you know her."

"I've known her ever since the third grade, when the teacher sat us beside each other. Logan and MacGregor." He shakes his head. "I was fifteen when I realized I had a crush. I spent so many years wondering why I wasn't into girls like my teammates were, why I wasn't so obsessed with getting into some chick's pants like them. It's deeper than that for me. I want more than sex with her. I want something real."

Squeezing his shoulder, I tell him, "I hope you get that."

"Just keep it out of the locker room." He laughs.

"Pretty much, yeah."

"Thanks, Cap," he says.

"For what it's worth, I think you two could be good for each other," I offer. "Just... talk to MacGregor, first. Before you make a move."

My teammate flinches. "Yeah. Okay. Cool. Totally not going to panic."

"There are things in life worthy of panicking over. This is not one of them." I squeeze his shoulder. "Go get your girl, Logan. Get your happily ever after."

Tilting his head, he studies me. "Did you?"

I flinch. "What do you mean?"

"I mean, with the divorce... Are you happy?"

Glancing out the window to my left, I catch another

glimpse of Amelia. She's curled up on the sofa now, Brandon holding the baby.

"I'm getting there," I tell him honestly.

"You know, you can talk to me," he says, so fucking earnest it makes my chest ache. "You listen to all of our bullshit and complaining. You're allowed to come to us with your own stuff, too."

"Thanks, man. I appreciate that."

Against my will, I look out the window again. This time, Logan follows my gaze.

"Holy fuck. Is that Amelia?"

"Yeah. We're neighbors," I say lamely. Like he couldn't figure it out on his own.

"That's neat," he says, taking it at face value. He waves at her, and she clocks the movement, smiling and waving back. "Well, I'll let you get back to whatever you were doing. Thanks for listening, McKittrick."

"Any time," I tell him. It's part of the job, after all.

"I'm here if you need anything."

I laugh. "Hey, that's my line."

"Yeah, but I actually mean it," Logan says. "Seriously. You want to talk, I'm your guy. Otherwise, I'll just pine obnoxiously for my best friend's sister."

sixteen

. . .

Amelia

AS THE SEASON GOES ON, we fall into a routine. The schedule is a cacophony of home games and road trips. When I'm in town, I spend as much time with my brothers as possible, soaking up all the baby snuggles, and resting when I can. Ainsley is growing so freaking fast, it's unbelievable.

Outside of the team, I haven't made any friends yet. But Robby, Joaquin, Patrice, and Vanessa keep my calendar plenty busy with brunch dates and drinks after work on non-game days. We always hang out when we're on the road. There's a camaraderie I didn't experience in Colorado or as an intern in Austin. Before, when the day was over, I left work behind. Now… it follows me wherever I go.

Maybe because I can see the team captain from my bedroom window each night. I haven't given him another show, not since our *session*, and if he's getting PT, it's from one of the other staff members because he hasn't been back on my table.

I've barely seen him. When we run into each other at the facility, he gives me a nod and keeps moving, and we haven't been in the same room for more than ten seconds before someone else walks in. There's no chance to talk about what happened.

He's giving me space. He deserves the courtesy of me giving him the same.

We have a whole two days off for Thanksgiving, so of course, the team gathers at our favorite dive bar for a night out. Some of the guys flew to their hometowns, but most of them brought their families here.

Brandon doesn't talk to his family, and Tyler isn't close to our dad, so it's just the three of us and Ainsley this year. We invited Robby to join us, and if he thinks it's weird to celebrate the holiday with his ex's husband, he hasn't mentioned it. Brandon said it would be weird if Robby were suddenly hanging out, but now, they're the best of friends.

Sven and Vanessa are also without extended families, but they politely declined our invitation. Patrice's mom and sisters came to visit, and Joaquin's brothers drove in from Rhode Island.

It's a lively crowd at the bar. The team fills the place, all the support staff also joining in. There is a much more fluid line between players and staff with the Grizzlies. On my past teams, there wasn't nearly as much mingling. I don't feel less than or inferior because I don't earn the big bucks, like they do.

Half the guys are younger than me, though there is a solid core of older veterans. Gonzo and Logan are my age, MacGregor is three years older, and Sinclair is right in there. McKittrick is the oldest player on the team.

I can't imagine what it's like, knowing your best days are behind you. He can still win the Cup, he still has another opportunity to push, but this is the last year of his contract. After spending the last eight years with Boston, who knows if they'll give him another. Who knows where he'll end up. The world is open to him, full of post-hockey opportunities.

But if I know McKittrick even half as well as I think I do,

he doesn't want a world post-hockey. He won't hang up his skates until he absolutely has to. He won't give up hockey until it's forcibly taken from him. I just hope it doesn't come to that.

Robby nudges me with his elbow, startling me from my introspection. "Why so glum, babe?"

"Just thinking." I sip my drink, letting the stringent flavor of the vodka flood my senses. "You good?"

The holidays can be rough when you have no contact with your family.

"I'm great," he says.

Looking him over, his eyes are a bit glassy, but he seems to be in control of his faculties.

"Really, Meels," he insists. "I'm desperately single, but unless you know a hot, single, queer man who doesn't have a U-Haul full of baggage, I'm doing good."

Laughing, I wrap my arm around him and squeeze him in a hug. "I don't, but I'll keep my eye out for you."

He sighs. "Yeah, thanks."

"Besides, I'm right there with you on the single front," I say before I can think better of it.

"Might I interest you in a no strings attached hookup?" He waves his hand in front of us. "Look at the buffet of hot, hopefully single, emotionally unavailable men. What's your type?"

"Not someone I work with."

Although...

Robby rolls his eyes. "Well, good thing we're in a bar full of people you don't know. I'll be your wingman, hype you up. Seriously, what's your type?"

"Tall. Dark hair."

"Right, right. Let's see what we can do." Chin in his hand, he scopes out the situation around us. "Lawyer?"

"Eh. I need someone who won't look down on me for my career, while also not being emasculated by the fact I spend my day surrounded by and touching half-dressed men."

"Good luck with that," he mutters.

"You're telling me."

"How do you feel about body hair?"

"Not opposed." I think of the way McKittrick's leg hair felt under my hand. I haven't seen him up close with his shirt off, only from a distance. But what I've seen… I definitely like.

"Build?"

"I like athletic, but I'm not opposed to someone who works a day job."

I care more about what's inside than outside.

Robby nods at a man in a well-fitting suit. He's a few inches short of six feet, but the confidence radiating from him makes me take a second glance. His full head of hair is chestnut brown and cut in a fashionable style. A light layer of scruff covers an impressive jawline.

"What do you think?" my friend mutters.

"He's hot," I admit, sipping my drink as I shamelessly check the guy out.

The man in question looks up, interest in his eyes.

… and then his gaze slips from me to Robby, his brows furrowing.

"Go for it, babe."

"I think he's more interested in you," I point out.

"Nah. He's just making sure I'm not competition." Robby gives me a light shove. "Go get 'im."

Shaking my head to hide a smile, I slip off the barstool and weave my way through the bar tables, like a woman on a mission. As I approach, the man turns to face me directly.

Fuck. He's even hotter up close.

"Hey." When my voice doesn't shake, I smile. "I'm Amelia."

"Sam," he says, in a clear, rich voice. "Your friend put you up to this?"

Laughing, I admit, "Something like that. Do you want to buy me a drink?"

His eyes drift over me, taking his time perusing me like a horse at auction, and I'm not certain how I feel about being considered merchandise.

"Sure," he says, turning back to the bar and flagging down the bartender. "What are you drinking?"

"Vodka and lemonade."

"Hmm. Interesting."

"Someone talked about it on a recipe blog once, and it sounded good. It's my go-to drink now."

When the bartender approaches, he orders, "A vodka and lemonade, please. And another gin and tonic for me." He hands over his card and the bartender scurries off to make the drinks.

An awkward silence falls between us.

"So, what do you do?" he asks.

"I'm a physical therapist."

"Oh, cool. I'm in tech consulting."

I don't know what that means. I'm half-convinced it's just a buzzword for *wasting people's time and money.*

But I know better than to say it out loud.

"Are you native to Boston?" I ask instead.

Sam shakes his head. "I did my MBA at Harvard. I'm originally from Albuquerque. You?"

"Military brat. I've lived all over. Born in London. My brothers live here, so I moved here."

His face falls. "You have brothers?"

"Yeah, two of them. They're great."

I don't mention that Brandon is a famous baseball player. More than once, guys have tried to use me to get to him.

"Hey, Amelia!"

McKittrick pops up behind Sam, a drink in his hand. As I

stand there, the hockey player sets an arm across my shoulders, leaning into me. He smells woodsy like pine, and I shouldn't like it as much as I do.

"What are you up to?" he asks.

"Talking to my friend here." I give him a sharp elbow to the ribs, expecting him to flinch away, but he only pulls me further into his side.

"Hey, man. I'm Jason."

"Sam." His eyes narrow as he glances between us. "Am I getting in the middle of something here?"

"Nope," I tell him brightly. "He was just leaving."

McKittrick doesn't take the hint. "Nice to meet you. Are you from around here?"

"Yeah, my place is around the corner."

"Cool, cool. We live in the financial district."

Sam cocks his head. "Both of you?"

"We're neighbors," I grit out.

"Yeah, it's pretty awesome," McKittrick adds.

The bartender sets our drinks in front of us, and I watch as Sam scribbles out a five percent tip. Hm. Not sure I can abide by that.

Reaching for my wallet, I withdraw a ten dollar bill and stuff it into the tip jar.

Sam's jaw clenches as his gaze darts from me to the jar. "Do you want to get out of here?"

"We just got our drinks." I sip from mine, ignoring McKittrick draped all over me. "Do you have anything fun planned for the weekend?"

"Nah, just working," he says. "I picked up a turkey dinner for one from the market."

"Oh."

"I'm hanging out with Meels, here," McKittrick says helpfully. "Her brother invited me."

"I didn't know that."

"Yeah. When Ty dropped off my meals for the week, we

talked about how my parents are with my sister this year at her in-laws. So, he invited me over."

"Huh," Sam says. "So, you guys really know each other."

McKittrick shrugs. "We work together, we live next door to each other… You could say we're best friends."

"We're not best friends," I hurry to add. "I barely know the guy."

"Yeah. Right." Sam gulps down his drink. "I'm going to get out of here. It was nice meeting you, Amy."

"It's *Amelia*," McKittrick stresses as Sam walks away.

I shove the hockey player off of me. "What the fuck was that?"

Why did I wait so long? I should have punched him the second he horned in on our conversation.

McKittrick sips his beer. "That was me saving you from a lifetime of boring."

My eyes narrow. "Excuse me?"

"He was boring as fuck."

"And what right do you have to—"

"I don't have any right," he says, with a shrug. "I saw someone that needed saving."

"I don't need *saving*. I can make my own decisions."

"Yeah, except when they're bad ones."

"I'm not looking for forever. I just want to get laid."

"Okay, then," McKittrick says. "Let's go back to my place."

"I'm not going sleeping with you!"

"If you insist." He shrugs, but there's tension in his shoulders. "I would never force you. All I'm saying is, you want one night of meaningless fun, you know where to find me."

"I—I—"

Letting out a chuckle, McKittrick steers me back to Robby. "If you change your mind, you know where I'll be."

seventeen

. . .

Jason

SHE DOESN'T KNOW what to make of me. I bet she never thought I'd actually *offer*. Fuck, *I* certainly never thought I'd say the words.

But Amelia Owen makes me do all sorts of things I never imagined doing.

From across the bar, I watch while she chats with Robby, Patrice, and Patrice's sister, and as the night draws to an end, I notice when she hefts her purse over her shoulder, like she's about to flee.

Striding through the dwindling crowd, I reach the exit right when she does.

"Heading home?" I ask, my phone in my hand to call a car.

"Yes." She glares at me. "Got something to say about it?"

"Wanna share a car? Mine is three minutes out."

Amelia rolls her eyes. "How convenient."

"It is, actually." As if it wasn't my plan all along. "We're going to the same place. I'm hardly forcing you to ride with me."

It's bitterly cold out, and as a burst of wind sweeps through the street, Amelia shivers in her coat.

"Fine," she bites out.

"You know, we never talked about it," I say casually.

"About being neighbors?"

"No. That day in the—"

"Shut up," she hisses, looking behind her, like one of our coworkers will magically appear there. "We aren't talking about that."

Stepping closer, I set my finger beneath her chin, tilting her head until she meets my gaze.

"Are we okay?"

She hesitates.

"Everything we did… We're okay? You don't regret it?"

"Not exactly." Her face flushes. "I just… we can't."

"Hey, I hear you, loud and clear. No more fooling around at work."

"Fuck," she whispers, her face flaming. "You can't just—"

"What about fooling around *outside* of work?"

She opens her mouth, and then closes it again. "It's a bad idea."

"Because we work together? Or because you don't want me?"

Amelia swallows. "The first one."

"Then, why do you show off for me?"

"You're the one who doesn't close the blinds," she says, her eyes flashing. "I wouldn't—"

"That first night, you knew I was there. Did you know who I was?"

She shakes her head. "I never saw anyone over there. Robby said you just moved in?"

I nod. "The day before."

She shivers, and I tug her into the circle of my arms, sharing my body heat. I'm on fire, and it's all because of her.

"Is it really that bad of an idea?" I ask.

"I like my job. I want to keep it." When I open my mouth,

she adds in, "I won't jeopardize my future for a fling. And that's all it would be."

"Why? Is it really that difficult to want to be with me?"

I can't help the bitterness coloring my tone. Harper thought I was too much of a hassle to deal with. *Inconvenient.*

But Amelia and I work together. She knows the score. She sees the insanity of my schedule firsthand.

"You just got divorced," she points out. "You can't seriously want to start something again."

Forcing a shrug, I say, "With you, I do."

Because it may have started out as only physical, but the truth is, I *like* Amelia. I want to spend time with her, even with our clothes on, have drinks with Andrews and the group, and share brunch with her brothers, and any other cutesy date-night thing couples do.

Was I expecting this to happen? No. The sight of her talking with that douchebag made me see red. It took everything in me not to kick his ass for looking at her like a piece of meat.

Am I ready for something serious? Maybe, maybe not. But I won't know unless I try.

Even when she's torturing me in PT, I enjoy my time with her... so much that I haven't gone into the medical suite without getting hard. I've relied on Zac and Graham to work on all my aches and pains. They don't boil my blood the way she does.

A sleek black car pulls up to the curb. "Jason?" the driver asks.

I nod, reaching for the door.

Amelia's hand lands on my arm. "Don't make this weird," she says quietly.

Searching her eyes, I find my nerves mirrored in them.

"I won't, if you won't," I tell her.

She nods, ducking into the car and scooting to the far side.

I slide in beside her, the gap of the empty middle seat a six-inch barrier that feels enormous.

We're both silent on the ten-minute ride back to our neighborhood. The driver has the local sports radio talk-show on in the background, running commentary on tonight's basketball game. The team loses more than they win; as a fellow Boston sports player, I understand how hard it is, but as a Boston sports *fan*, their downward spiral this season is hard to watch.

Before long, the car pulls up to our block, and after I get out, I hold the door open for Amelia.

"Is this where we say goodnight?" I ask. "I'm fine if—"

"Shut up," she snaps, brushing her hair into a ponytail, which she secures with the scrunchie around her wrist. "Take me upstairs, fuck me stupid, and let's never talk about it again."

My mouth snaps shut. "Okay."

A satisfied smirk settles on her face. I'd like to satisfy her in a thousand other ways.

Tim, the doorman, opens the door as we approach.

"Good evening, Mr. McKittrick," he says, with a nod. "Miss."

"Have a good night, Tim," I say, patting his shoulder as we pass.

The guard behind the desk, Paul, opens the residents' only door for us. I nod at him when we pass through, and then wave my fob at the elevator bay.

"You have a lot of security," Amelia comments.

"It's one reason so many of the players live here. We don't have to worry." As the elevator doors open and I punch the button for the nineteenth floor, I add, "Don't you have just as much security?"

"Yeah, but I'm nobody. It's all for Brandon."

I shrug. "Sure, but you get the benefits."

She turns to me, crossing her arms over her chest. "Do you really want to talk about my brother right now?"

The elevator doors open on my floor. "Not really."

My apartment is at the end of the hall. Opening the door, I usher her inside.

She unbuttons her coat, looking around the place curiously. I take it in with fresh eyes, the leather sofa and bare, off-white walls.

"What do you think?"

Across the way, her apartment is dark. There's no sign of her brothers.

"Looks different from this angle." She tosses her coat against the armchair. "Can you do me a favor?"

"Yeah, anything." Fuck, did my voice come out as breathless as it felt? What is she doing to me?

Amelia grins. "Close the blinds."

Crossing the room, I do as she requested.

She stalks across the room, her steps sure as she approaches me. I turn around right when she reaches me, and before I know it, her mouth is on mine.

She tastes like lemonade and sunshine, her lips yielding under mine. Electricity simmers beneath my skin, ready to overtake me.

I don't have any answers. I don't know what this is, or what it could be. Whether either of us are ready for it. All I know is, she's the only thing on my mind, and not a day goes by that I don't want more. Crave more. *Need* more.

One time with Amelia wasn't enough. A second hit won't quell the fire burning inside me. I'll need her all the time, and I don't ever want to stop.

She tugs at the hem of my T-shirt, and I break the kiss to pull it off, tossing the cotton behind me. When I go to kiss her again, she pulls back, her hand landing on my chest.

"I didn't get to look before," she says, her palm skating over my pec. My skin erupts with goosebumps, the feeling of her skin on mine sending dangerous thoughts through my head.

Want. Need. Claim.

Her fingertips trail down my abs, brushing over the bruise on my obliques, and she drags her nails through the coarse hair covering my belly. Does she like it? I overheard her and Andrews talking about body hair, but not enough to know her preference. Should I have shaved it off? Waxed?

Whatever she wants, I'll do it. All she has to do is look at me with those big, brown doe eyes, and I'm putty for her.

Amelia reaches for my belt, making quick work of the leather, and pulling it free. She wraps the strap around her fist, and my cock jerks so fast, it makes me dizzy.

I've always been the assertive one. I've always been in charge. In hockey, in relationships, I've always had control because there's never been anyone I trusted enough to let go with.

But when she hooks a finger in the waistband of my jeans and tugs me forward, I'm powerless for the first time, and I fucking love it. She walks backwards until the back of her legs hit the couch, and then she twists and pushes me down.

I reach for her, with intent to pulling her onto my lap, but she has other ideas.

"No touching," she says, her eyes bright.

"Or what?" My voice is rough as sandpaper, and I rub my sweaty palms on my thighs.

"Or this stops."

Amelia backs up a few steps, her movements graceful, and she picks up her phone. In short order, she connects to the speaker, a soft jazz tune playing throughout the room.

Her fingers trail down her torso, drawing my gaze to her delicious curves. She's wearing a simple v-neck sweater and dark jeans, the denim clinging to her hips and ass. Her body sways to the music as she lifts the hem of her sweater a few inches.

"Yes. Take it off."

Dark eyes flashing, she does as I ask, the dark blue fabric

landing in a heap behind her. Underneath, she's wearing a simple tank top, the soft pink straps of her bra visible beneath. I wonder if it's the same lacy pink one I saw in her hotel room.

My cock twitches at the memory of waking up beside her, her warm body cocooning mine. I felt safe in a way I never experienced before. Despite being disoriented and hungover, I never once worried about someone finding out or, worse, doing something I can't take back with the wrong person. Because with her, I'm safe.

Her tank top goes next, landing on the floor beside her sweater. The lacy, light pink bra does a miraculous job showcasing her full breasts. Her fingertips trace along the cup of the bra, drawing my eyes, and as all remaining blood in my brain rushes south, she pulls her hand away.

Amelia pops the buttons on her jeans, slowly peeling them off her hips. My hands curl into fists on my thighs, desperately wanting to touch. Her. Myself. Both. I don't know.

Stepping out of her jeans, she twists, and I catch a glimpse of her ass, encased in black cotton panties. With her back to me, her arms stretch above her head, highlighting the length of her spine.

A groan escapes my lips. I'm sweating, my heart pounding. This is simultaneously the best and worst night of my life. Best, because it's with her. Worst, because I can't fucking *touch* her.

Her hands move to the clasp of her bra, letting it fall to the floor, and then she steps out of her panties. The curve of her bare ass is right fucking there, and I can't do anything about it.

Turning to face me again, I get my first glance of Amelia up close and personal. My mouth goes dry, and I'm fairly certain my eyes bug out.

"You like what you see?" she asks, playing with her hair.

"I'm not sure."

Her confident smile fades.

"Come here. I need a closer look."

She steps toward me, her hand landing on my bare shoulder, and she climbs onto my lap.

"Mm. Much better," I say, before threading my hand through her ponytail. Gripping the strands, I pull her closer, and as our mouths collide again, all is right with the world.

eighteen

. . .

Amelia

HOLY FUCK, McKittrick can kiss. I thought I knew what he could do after our encounter the other day, but this kiss… it's electric. Heat simmers in my veins, just beneath the surface. His tight grip on my ponytail doesn't give me an inch, and as his other hand skates over my curves, I start to tremble. I want him so fucking badly, it almost hurts.

His fingers trail over the crease of my hip, and then between my legs. When he feels the slickness there, his lips curve into a smirk against mine.

"Shut up," I murmur into the kiss.

"I didn't say anything," he says, before driving two fingers inside me.

My eyes flutter shut, sensory overload overwhelming my system. It takes a second for my brain to come back online, and every time he thrusts his fingers into me, little zaps of pleasure fry my brain. All of my synapses are firing at full speed and then some, flooding my bloodstream with pleasure.

I'm forced to break the kiss, burying my face in his neck and breathing in his woodsy scent. The scrape of his scruff against my cheek grounds me, offering me a lifeline.

When his thumb brushes my clit, I clench around him, and he lets out a dark chuckle.

"Feel good?" he murmurs, his face buried in my hair.

"Shut up," I say again.

"Talk to me. Tell me how you're feeling." He strums my clit, knowing exactly how to play my body.

"Can't. Talk."

"Oh? Should I stop?" He pulls his fingers free, and I whine, grabbing for his hand and dragging his fingers back to where I want them. He runs them through my folds, withholding what I need most.

"Close."

"Tell me what you need."

"I need you to touch me." Breathing hard, I force myself upright. I'm so worked up, I'm almost dizzy. "I need your fingers inside me."

"Yes, ma'am," McKittrick says, a smirk on his lips. I want to slap it off.

But I'm not about non-consensual spanking, so I settle for kissing it away.

His fingers thrust inside me, curling until they find the spot that drives me crazy. I clench around him, grinding my clit against the palm of his hand.

My breaths come faster now, and when he bites at my lips and then soothes the sting with his tongue, I moan.

"Say my name."

"Mc—"

He shakes his head. "Say my *name*, Amelia."

"Jason."

"Again."

"Jason."

"Good girl."

Something inside me lights up at his praise. I want to be a good girl. I want to be *his* good girl.

His grip tightens in my hair, and it's that simple sensation that tips me over the edge.

My entire body lights up with pleasure, bright white lights bursting behind my eyelids.

As I come down, Jason's kiss gentles, his lips tethering me to this plane of existence. Once the aftershocks fade, he pulls his fingers free. I collapse against his strong chest, my eyes fluttering shut as I try to regulate my breathing.

His strong arms wrap around me, and before I know what's happening, I'm airborne. My legs wrap around his waist as he carries me into the bedroom, kicking the door shut behind him.

He lays me out on the center of the bed, pausing only to drop his pants and briefs before he crawls onto the bed.

But he doesn't stretch out beside me.

No, he stops halfway up the bed, spreading my legs. I start to close them, but he forces them open, gazing at me.

And when he dips his head, tasting me for the first time, my eyes nearly roll back into my head. He settles my legs over his shoulders, and my hands slide into his hair. It's as soft as I imagined, the strands the perfect length to grip.

Jason isn't shy, his touch sure as he devours me. His fingers slide home inside me, intent on wringing every ounce of pleasure from my body.

And when I break for the second time, the satisfaction on his face mirrors mine.

He finally joins me against the pillows, and he pulls me into his arms, resting my head on his pecs. The coarseness of his chest hair abrades my cheek in the best possible way.

I've been single by choice for a *long* time. It's hard to find a man who isn't intimidated by my career or the people I hang out with. And it's even more difficult to find someone who can abide by my schedule, the constant travel wreaking havoc on a relationship.

It's easier to focus on one night only situations. But those don't typically lend themselves to cuddling, to being held in a man's arms.

Jason's legs tangle with mine, his body wrapped around me.

As I recover, I trail my hand over his chest, down his abs, and further to his cock, standing at attention and digging into my hip. I start to think that maybe this doesn't have to be a one night only thing.

The connection between us is electric. He knows it just as well as I do. Why should our jobs dictate who we sleep with?

His hand drives into my hair, twisting the strands around his fingers as he holds me close to him. The way he kisses me… He knows we only have tonight. So, why am I worrying about a nebulous future? I should enjoy what we have now. No need to borrow tomorrow's trouble.

My hand wraps around his cock, giving him a firm stroke. He's hot and hard in my hand, smooth as velvet, with sticky pre-cum easing the glide of my strokes. I use my other hand to cup his balls, rolling them.

He shudders, his hands mapping over my skin, the swell of my breasts, the curve of my hip. He's touching me like he can't get enough, and I have to admit, the idea goes to my head a bit. I haven't felt desired in a long time. I haven't felt *desirable*.

I don't regretted being a surrogate, but for the last year, I lost sight of who I am. Between all the hormones before the implantation and then the pregnancy weight, it's taken a while to feel like myself again. To feel like a woman and not just an incubator.

But now? There's no doubting the want in his eyes, in his touch.

My body did something incredibly powerful, and yes, it doesn't look the same as before. I have stretch marks and battle scars. My hips are wider, my breasts fuller. I can't take it back.

And *I'm* not the same as before. I'm irrevocably changed.

Jason trails his thumb over my cheek, his eyes searching mine, and I realize my hand stilled on his cock when I was lost in thought.

"You with me?" he murmurs.

"I am now."

"We don't have to do this." He's so fucking earnest, like his cock isn't throbbing in my fist. "If you're not into it…"

"That's not what it is. I was—it doesn't matter. I'm here. I'm focused." Giving him a sultry smile, I resume stroking him. "Do you have a condom?"

He moves my hand off his cock. "Maybe we should talk about whatever's bothering you."

"It's not bothering me." But taking the hint, I roll away from him, intent on getting out of the bed. If we aren't having sex, I definitely don't want a heart-to-heart conversation with him.

But Jason follows me, molding his body against my back. His erection presses into my ass, but he doesn't make any attempt to grind it into me. He wraps his arm around my torso, his hand on my ribcage, just beneath my breasts.

"Talk to me, Amelia."

"I just… thoughts. I had thoughts."

He presses a kiss on the back of my neck. "Bad thoughts?"

"No. They were… insecurities. Things I don't really want to verbalize right now."

Or ever.

"How can I reassure you? How can I prove that I want you?"

"You could fuck me."

He goes still.

"Amelia…"

"Fuck me stupid, actually, is what I asked for." I heave an exaggerated sigh. "But if you don't want to follow through…"

His hand slides from my ribs to between my legs, cupping me there.

"That's not what this is. Not at all."

"Then, what is it?"

"I don't want to do this, if you're not into it." Jason strokes his fingers through my folds, but makes no attempt to enter me. "I don't want empty, meaningless sex. I want *you*."

Carefully, I turn in the circle of his arms.

"Then, fuck me," I whisper.

His lips crash down onto mine, and it's just as electric as every other kiss has been. He gets under my skin, digging in and pressing on all of my insecurities.

With a gasp, he breaks the kiss, then rolls away. Rummaging in the nightstand, he comes up with a condom and a bottle of lube. As I watch, he suits up, and then liberally applies the lube. I'm plenty wet, but there's no such thing as too much lube. And given it's been a while for me…

I move to the center of the bed, and he joins me there, his cock bobbing. He notches the head at my entrance, and I tense.

He freezes. "What is it?"

Swallowing, I admit, "It's my first time since Ainsley. Just… go slow."

His face softens. "Always."

Dropping forward onto his elbows, he kisses me, slow and deep. And when I finally relaxed, melting into him, he slides inside me. I wrap my arms around him, burying my face in his neck. His scent immediately calms my racing heart, his body a weighted blanket soothing my overstimulated synapses.

Ohhhhh fuck. This is even better than I imagined. My cunt pulses around him, adjusting to his size. He gives me time to breathe through it.

Our bodies are connected in the most intimate way possible, but it's more than the physicality of it. It's more than pure, unbridled lust. Sure, we have that in spades. All he's offering me is one night; I don't get any more of him. Not if I want to keep my job.

But as he fucks me with firm, steady strokes, it becomes more and more difficult to remember why that's so important. Financial independence? A healthy self-worth? Who needs those things when I can spend all my time being speared by the hockey captain's massive cock? I could be his on-demand cock sleeve, ready and waiting in his bed at all hours of the day.

It's a fantasy. It's not real life. It's not something I want for myself, even in the deepest confines of my mind. It's fun to think about, but I'm not cut out for a true submissive sexual connection.

Jason lifts my hips off the bed, supporting my body weight and changing the angle until he hits the spot that makes me moan, my skin breaking out in goosebumps.

"There it is," he murmurs, his lips brushing my temple.

His hands skate over my body, playing with my nipples, brushing my clit, fisting my ass. He doesn't stop touching me, his reverence sending butterflies fluttering in my belly.

"I—"

I don't know what to say. I have no words. They're all gone. Poof. He's stolen my ability for rational thought, and I'm not even upset about it.

My hands move from his shoulders to his chest, down the ladder of his abs, and further to where we're connected. As my fingers brush my clit and the base of his shaft, he stiffens, and I can't hide my pleased smile.

"Oh, no, you don't," he says, nudging my hand away.

And then he touches me, his thumb moving in determined circles around my clit. I'm teetering on the edge, every fiber of my being stretched tight, like an elastic at its limit.

Pulling him onto me, his chest hair brushing my breasts, his hand trapped between our bodies, I finally snap.

"Jason," I gasp, and he lets out a growl of satisfaction that rumbles through me.

I unravel in his arms, and he fucks me through it, his steady strokes faltering. It's not until I collapse back against the pillows that he takes his own pleasure, fucking me so hard the headboard rattles against the wall.

"Come for me." I run my hand through his hair, and when I cup his cheek, he presses it into my palm.

Two thrusts later, his entire body tenses, the veins in his neck raised in stark relief. His cock jerks inside of me, emptying into the condom.

Pulling out and still breathing hard, he collapses beside me, his hand reaching out to thread his fingers through mine.

"That was…" I have no words.

"Yeah."

We lay there in silence for a moment, the only sound in the room our ragged breathing.

After a few minutes, he rolls out of bed. I turn my head to watch as he pads to the bathroom, dealing with the condom and cleaning up. Even though I need to get up, I need to go home, I'm not ready for this to be over.

Jason returns with a wet washcloth, steam rising from the terrycloth. My stomach clenches at the idea he warmed it up for me, rather than running the cold tap. I go to take it, but he shakes his head, taking care to clean me up before tossing the washcloth onto the nightstand.

"C'mere," he murmurs, pulling me into his arms.

"I should go home."

"Okay," he says, tightening his arms around me. "Just not yet."

nineteen

. . .

Jason

HERE'S THE THING: when you're at the Thanksgiving table the day after the best sex of your life, surrounded by her friends and family, things get… messy. And confusing.

Because my night with Amelia blows every other experience I've had out of the water. Every past partner, even my ex-wife… none of them hold a candle to her.

And I don't know if that's because it can't happen again, or if we really are that explosive together, but either way, we can't do it again. It pisses me the fuck off. I spent years being miserable in a dead-end marriage. Years telling myself I would see my commitments through, no matter how they made me feel.

Then Harper served me with divorce papers. She had the courage to take the step I couldn't. And I'm so fucking grateful for that, every single day.

But I can't keep putting my life on hold.

I want Amelia. She wants me. Why can't we make a go of this? Why should a little thing like our jobs get in the way of us being happy together?

Tyler invited me for the holiday in good faith. He probably didn't expect me to go and sleep with his sister. But the connection we shared… It's worth the awkwardness today.

Amelia snuck out of my bed around dawn. She wasn't trying to wake me, but I'm a light sleeper, and when I lost the warmth against my back was gone, it startled me. I'm not sure how we got into that position again, with me as the little spoon, considering we fell asleep in the other direction, but I have to admit I liked it.

We don't know each other well, but I feel safe with her. I trust her.

From the safety of my bed, I watched as she entered her own room. She waved, undressed, and climbed into bed. I fell back asleep with a smile on my face.

When I woke up again, her room was empty, and there was a single text on my phone. *Don't make this weird.* The same thing she said before she got in the car. Before she came home with me and irrevocably changed my life.

I'm doing my fucking best.

She's wearing a simple red dress, the material clinging to her curves. Her dark hair is pulled back with a white sequined bow. It should look silly, like a little girl playing dress up, but there's no denying Amelia is all woman. There's nothing innocent about her, especially not after last night.

When I show up at her door, she blinks, but lets me in without questioning my presence.

Inside, Andrews is on the sofa across from Brandon and another man. Austin Anderson. He's a pitcher for the Bulldogs, and a damn good one, too. We met two or three previous times at a charity function or golf tournament.

Over the next hour, two more baseball players arrived with their partners. Holcomb I've met before, Jackson I haven't. I'm the lone hockey player, but I don't feel left out. Andrews and I are polite, maybe even friendly, and Brandon is nothing but welcoming.

As we sit at the table, I maneuver my way casually through the crowd until I can sit next to Amelia.

But I didn't think about how torturous it would be to sit beside her all afternoon while not being able to touch her.

Tyler sits at the head of the table, Brandon beside him, and Ainsley in a high chair between them. She's too young for solids, but she can sit with us.

There's no blessing over the food, and we don't go around the table forcing people to say what they're thankful for. That's always my least favorite part of the day. It never feels genuine; it's always coerced, especially given the origination of the holiday.

Tyler outdid himself. The turkey is beautiful, carved to perfection, and the table is groaning under the weight of the sides.

Beside me, Amelia sets her hand on my arm. "Jase—" She snaps her mouth shut.

Andrews blinks at her. "What did you just say?"

She shakes her head. "McKittrick. Will you pass the potatoes?"

"No. You were about to call him something else." His eyes narrow. "Since when are you two on a first-name basis?"

I doubt he'd like the real answer.

But I pass her the potatoes, holding the bowl as she scoops some onto her plate.

"Last night, he introduced himself to that guy as Jason. I guess it stuck." Her face flushes. "I get why you didn't want him to know your last name or what you do."

"What guy?" Ty asks, his voice sharp.

"At the bar. I tried to hit on a guy, and it didn't go well," she says. Her cheeks are definitely red now. "*McKittrick* stepped in and saved me. The dude was a total dud."

"Sorry, babe," Andrews says, clucking his tongue. "We'll find someone else for you."

My stomach churns at the idea of Amelia and yet another guy. I want her to be with me—and only me.

"I'm sure I'll manage just fine," she says. "Besides, we're about to leave on a five day road trip."

Five days. We'll be together for five days. Five nights in hotels.

Five nights surrounded by the entire team and all of our support staff.

Fuck.

"What do you do?" Anderson asks. He's the only other single and presumably straight male at the table. The other two ball players brought partners. Of course, he's interested in her. Who wouldn't be?

"I'm a physical therapist for the Grizzlies," she says.

He lets out a low whistle. "Impressive job, keeping those guys in line."

The hairs on the back of my neck raise. "What's that supposed to mean?"

Anderson shakes his head. "You guys play a physical, demanding sport. Our PTs and athletic trainers are so busy, and we have minimal contact. I can't imagine what it takes to maintain peak condition for the entirety of a season."

"Yes, yes, hockey is the superior sport," Andrews says flippantly. He was a goaltender until he busted his knee. He played a few games in the big leagues, but spent most of his time in the minors before he got injured.

I wonder if that's how he met Tyler and Amelia. I've always wanted to know, but never asked.

"But have you seen the baseball pants?" he continues. "I should have figured out I was queer when I spent more time looking at the players' asses than at their swings."

"How do you think I snagged this one?" Brandon says, hitching his thumb toward his husband. "It's the ass."

"Hockey butts are better," Amelia says, matter of fact.

My chest swells with heat. I knew she was checking me out.

"How do you know what hockey players' butts look like?" Tyler demands.

She blinks. "It's literally my job. I see them and touch them all day long."

Sagging with disappointment, I do my best to keep my expression clear. Even if it's her job, I don't want to be lumped in with the rest of the guys. I know nothing inappropriate is going on with the rest of the team.

But it only serves to highlight how inappropriate it is for *us* to be together.

If the three straight baseball players are put off by the conversation, they don't show it.

"It's the forearms for me," says Holcomb's wife. He's a shortstop. "I could watch the forearms all day."

Holcomb flushes. "Babe."

"What? You're hot. Flaunt it while you've still got it."

Amelia reaches for the wine bottle, topping off her glass, and then offering it to me. I shake my head. I've already had two, and I have a matinee game tomorrow. I already know I'll regret eating such a heavy meal, despite how delicious it is.

Settling back in my chair, my hand falls to my full stomach. "Thank you for inviting me."

Brandon laughs. "Well, what's the alternative, you sit in your apartment and watch us having fun without you?"

My face flushes. It's the truth. I would have eaten one of Tyler's prepared meals with the football game on in the background, desperately wishing I could join them.

It's not being alone. That doesn't bother me. It's *them*.

Her.

The love the Owen siblings share is tangible. Brandon slots into their family so perfectly that I can't imagine him not being part of their dynamic. Even Andrews, despite being Tyler's ex, fits in so seamlessly.

I don't have that. I'm not close to my parents or my siblings. They're proud of me, but they have their own lives, spouses, kids, and jobs, and I have… hockey.

But lately, I've started to think about what comes next. When I don't have hockey anymore, what will I be left with? An empty condo, a busted knee, and virtually no friends. Sure, I have my teammates—for now. But once I'm done, they may not want to hang out. When I'm not their captain, will they still have time for me?

What will I do when I don't have hockey to define me anymore? Who will I be? The entire world is open to me. I can do anything. And it's overwhelming as fuck.

For now, I still have this season. I don't have to figure it out right this minute. I can worry about it later.

twenty

. . .

Amelia

SNOW BLANKETS the ground in Buffalo. Despite my winter boots, I'm slipping and sliding on the slick pavement as I haul my equipment bag into the arena. The boys won yesterday's home game, and now we have a full day of practice and workouts before a night off. After the game tomorrow night, we're on the road to Ottawa before finishing the road trip with a stop in Montreal.

I follow Derek and Graham into the arena and to our medical bay. The guys will start rolling in for their yoga class in about an hour, so I have plenty of time to get set up.

There's a knock on the door, and I look up to find Robby in the threshold, two cups of coffee in his hands.

"How're you doing?" he asks, offering me one.

"I'm good. Slept like shit." I take the paper cup and blow on the opening before taking a sip, even though I know it'll scald my tongue.

It does. It fucking hurts. But the caffeine warms me from the inside out, and sometimes, that's worth a burned tongue.

"Oh? Any reason why?" He raises an eyebrow expectantly.

"Because someone set the alarm clock in the room to go off at four o'clock in the fucking morning, and I wasn't smart enough to turn it off before I went to sleep."

"Oh? Not any… extracurricular activities?"

I roll my eyes. Whatever he's trying to insinuate, I won't play his game.

"No, I didn't pack my vibrator." Only on domestic trips—not international. I don't want to get stopped by customs agents and have to explain my *equipment* in front of the guys.

"Shame. You could probably use a good fucking," Robby drawls.

My eyes narrow.

"You know, since you're so tense."

"I'm not *tense*."

"Really? You seem tense."

"Stop saying tense." I take another sip of coffee so I don't give in to the urge to hurl it in his stupid, pretty face.

"Or maybe you recently got a good fucking," he says slowly, raising his eyebrows.

"I don't know what you're talking about."

"Really? Because I seem to remember you and *Jason* leaving the bar together."

"He was already leaving when I went outside. We shared a car home. We live on the same block."

"Uh huh."

"That's it. Nothing happened."

Except it was *everything*. That night… I've relived it in my head over and over, making myself come to the memory of him in me, on me, and surrounding me.

It was more than just sex. But to him, that's all it was.

And it's not like it will ever happen again. I value my career too much to throw it away for a fling… no matter how hot the sex is.

Robby looks me up and down, clearly not buying it.

"When you're ready to tell me, you will," he says confidently. "I trust he won't get wasted and need help back to the hotel tonight?"

"I'm not the teams' keeper. I don't know where he or the rest of the guys are going."

He hums. "Sure, you don't."

"Patrice talked about this dive bar on First Street," I mention to deflect the conversation. "It sounds good."

"I'm always down for a dive bar." He gives me one last scrutinizing look. "It would be okay, you know? If you did have a thing for him."

I roll my eyes. "I don't have *a thing* for him."

"Just… take care of yourself." He squeezes my arm. "He has a lot of shit going on. I hope he can give you what you need."

"Right now, what I need is you getting out of my space." I only have a few minutes before Jenkins shows up.

To my surprise, Robby envelops me in a hug. "Love you, Meels," he murmurs into my hair.

With a sigh, I sink into him. "Love you, too, Robby."

He means well, misguided as he is. There's nothing between me and Jason. It was one night. That's all it was. That's all it will ever be.

———

Buffalo won't give us an inch. I'm in the tunnel with the rest of the staff, clustered together to watch the action a few feet away. It's the middle of the third period, and the boys are *rowdy*. They don't like being down two goals, and they especially don't like three penalty kills in seven minutes.

And only one of those was actually Jenkins' fault. The other two were circumstantial at best, the result of sloppy play and lack of discipline. The situation is getting dicey, and that means someone's about to get hurt. Hopefully, it'll be someone on the other team, and not one of my players.

Derek is the tape and glue guy; he patches together what he can, and Doctor Hudson will stitch any facial injuries, if it comes to that. My job is more of the recovery and maintenance variety than acute treatment. For most of what I do, the patient has to rest and ice first before I can assess the damage and put together a plan of attack.

The game is getting chippy, and the chirps are decidedly less than polite. I don't know what Jenkins did to draw the ire of the entire Buffalo bench, aside from existing, because they've been after him all night long. When he finally snapped and tripped Hastings, it was entirely justified.

Well—mostly.

Hockey is still a team sport, and he's letting his frustration get the better of him rather than let the team shut Hastings down.

Mainly because the team as a whole is failing to shut *anything* down. MacGregor loses the face-off, and the Buffalo forward passes the puck to Hastings.

Logan tries to block him and deflect the play, but Hastings saucers the puck across the ice. McKittrick tries to get a stick on it, but his poke check only succeeds in poking Hastings' skates, and the opposing forward falls to the ice.

The ref blows the whistle and calls the penalty. Tripping.

Fuck.

The staffers in my immediate vicinity sigh and groan as the Buffalo stands erupt with cheers.

McKittrick is *pissed.* He skates to the penalty box with murderous intent on his face.

Coach Turner calls a time out, but as the players huddle around the clipboard, my eyes are on the captain across the ice.

He's stewing in his frustration, his face red from anger

and exertion. His dark hair is soaked with sweat, and even from across the arena, I can see the way how wild his dark eyes are, darting around the ice like a caged animal.

It's only two minutes.

The ref blows the whistle, signaling the time out has ended, and I watch as Larsson, MacGregor, Logan, and Sinclair take the ice, ready to kill off the captain's penalty.

They're mostly successful. They keep Buffalo on their toes for one minute and forty-seven seconds.

And then when Logan clears the puck, it ends up right on the tape of fucking Hastings, and the asshole snipes a shot on goal.

Luckily, Henry's on top of it, kicking out with his pad to deflect the shot. But he isn't fast enough to control the rebound, and another Buffalo player—I can't see his name from here—cleans it up, firing left side high.

The puck goes straight into the back of the net, the lamp lights up, and the entire bench deflates.

Three to zero, Buffalo.

McKittrick slams his helmet onto his head, striding out onto the ice. He doesn't get in place for the face-off; no, he goes straight to the bench, where Coach proceeds to harangue him until both of them are red in the face.

The hockey player jerks his head in a nod, his entire posture stiff. Tension sets into his shoulders, and I know deep in the pit of my stomach that this isn't good.

When the shifts change and McKittrick is back on the ice, he's immediately cross-checked by Hastings.

McKittrick tumbles to the ground in an awkward heap, his helmet clanging loudly against a stanchion in the boards, and my blood runs cold.

Oh, no. No, no, no.

He's on the ground for three, four, five seconds, before the refs blow the whistle and call the play dead. Derek strides forward, Lewis opening the gate for him, and Jenkins and

Easton escort he head athletic trainer onto the ice. The two players glide him down to the opposite end of the ice, where the captain lays in a crumpled heap.

But he's getting up!

McKittrick forces himself to a sitting position, and then uses his stick to balance. Derek hovers over him, talking to him, and McKittrick must say the right thing, because Derek nods and helps him up.

Hunched over with his stick across his knees, McKittrick is breathing hard, but I can see that he's in pain. A lot of it.

My heart hammers rapid-fire in my chest, like it's me who's under attack. Everything in me freezes solid, fear rooting me to the spot.

McKittrick reaches the gate, limping down the chute to the dressing room. I don't know what to say. Do I say anything?

"Amelia," Derek barks. "You're my eyes out here."

"You got it," I say, saluting him.

Right. I have to work. I have to focus.

If anything else happens tonight, I'm on deck. Not that anything will happen. There is only seven minutes left in the period, and—

Oh, *fuck*.

Jenkins and Hastings are fighting.

Reaching into my med bag, I pull out an ice pack and a clean towel, knowing I'll need it in approximately three point six seconds.

And when Hastings lands a right hook to Jenkins' face, it's over. The two fall to the ice, grappling with each other, until the refs break up the fight. Jenkins gets sent to the bench for repairs, while Larsson takes his spot in the sin bin, serving his teammate's penalty.

I hold the ice pack to Jenkins' knuckles, which are busted and bloody.

"What the fuck, kid," I mutter, inspecting his face. He's

sweaty and flushed, but aside from a bruise blooming on his cheek, he doesn't appear broken.

"He had it coming," the rookie mutters.

"Gotta learn you can't punch above your weight," Easton says, clapping him on the shoulder. "Good tilly, though. Has to happen sometimes."

"I led the AHL in PIMs," Jenkins mutters. Penalty Infraction Minutes.

He bounced around the minors for the last two years, but it seems like he's in the big club for a while. If this didn't change the team's perception of him, that is.

"Well, you're not in the AHL anymore, you're in the NHL now, and we do things a little differently here," Easton says. He shakes his head. "Welcome to the show, rookie."

The remaining few minutes of the game wind down, scoreless on our side, and the somber team makes their way into the dressing room.

I head straight for the medical bay, where I write up a brief about Jenkins' hand. I'm just finalizing the report on my tablet when footsteps make me look up.

When he's on the ice, he's McKittrick, but when he's alone in here with me, he's Jason. I can't go back to last names after he was inside of me. Consumed me.

And right now, I don't think he even recognizes that I'm here. He slams the door shut, and then throws his helmet across the room. It clangs off a cabinet, and he slams his fist against the door, punching twice. He sweeps an arm across a tray of medical supplies, sending them clattering to the floor. He looks around the room, eyes wild and unseeing, until he sags against the door, breathing hard.

Out there, he's a fierce competitor, insanely stubborn. With me, he'll find he doesn't need to be so fucking stoic all the time. He can feel his feelings, whether he's ready to do it with an audience or not.

When he doesn't move, I clear my throat. "Are you done?"

He jumps, whirling around to face me. "What are you doing here?"

"I work here." Setting my tablet aside, I face him. "Do you want to talk about it?"

Jason scowls. "No."

"Okay. Well, if you ever change your mind, you know where to find me."

twenty-one

. . .

Jason

I DO KNOW where to find her. She's at the front of the plane on our flight to Ottawa, chatting with Joaquin and Patrice. She's at the staff table in the meeting room, eating with Robby and Graham. She's seven doors down from me in the hotel, consuming my every thought.

And she's in the medical bay, the PT on staff today. I can't avoid her forever. I almost want to skip PT, but my knee will only hurt more if I do.

I want her, but after she saw me break down… I don't know if she still feels the same way. If she ever did.

I knock on the open door. She looks up, and her smile fades when she catches sight of me, her face going carefully blank.

"How's your knee?" she asks.

"Fine."

I'm lucky I didn't get a concussion when I fell awkwardly into the boards. Tweaking my bad knee is already a problem.

Amelia crosses her arms over her chest. "If you're fine, why're you here?"

She knows me far too well.

With a sigh, I sag against the doorframe. "Regular maintenance."

"Right." She picks up her tablet, flicking through the apps. "No acute injury, no sprains. Your x-ray was fine."

"Well, I don't *feel* fine."

She blows out a breath, gesturing me inside. "Close the door."

I limp into the room, and heave myself onto the table. My knee throbs when I stretch out, every pulse of my blood echoing in my ears.

Snapping on a pair of gloves, Amelia approaches, her eyes sweeping over my legs. I have a bruise on my left shin and a cut on my right ankle, but my knee isn't swollen or red. It looks normal to me. It just fucking *aches.*

Her hands, cold even through the latex, land on my skin, and I jump. She presses on the base of my femur, above the knee socket and below the joint, testing it. The light pressure makes my knee throb, and I let out a hiss.

"Bad?" she asks, her voice a soft murmur.

"Not great."

"Well, it could be the osteoarthritis acting up," she says. "There's nothing structurally wrong."

Scrubbing a hand over my face, I sigh. "Wonderful. Great."

"I'll do an athletic massage, if you think it will help."

"I honestly don't know what will help."

"Rest. Take a game off, ice and elevate, and we'll assess the day after tomorrow."

Scoffing, I tell her, "I won't take a game off."

Amelia shrugs. "I can't force you to. It's not my call. If Derek and Doc Hudson think you can play, go for it."

"Then, why did you say to rest it?"

"Because sometimes, they forget there's more to life than hockey. You have another fifty years ahead of you. What will you do when you want to run around after your kids, but can't because your knee acts up?"

"I don't want kids," I say immediately, and I'm surprised to find it's true.

For years, I was ambivalent. It helped that my ex-wife was firmly in the child-free mindset. All the power to her, but I thought I might want a kid one day.

But now... I don't think I do. And a kid isn't something you can be *kind of sure* about. You have to be certain. They have to be wanted. And I... don't want that life.

I wouldn't have a problem if my hypothetical child was queer or disabled or thought differently than me. Having a child isn't like going to Build-A-Bear; you can't pick out their attributes ahead of time. They'll have their own personality. And what if their personality doesn't jibe with mine? What if they're an extrovert? I can barely deal with the social demands of being captain.; I couldn't manage being "on" all the time. I need my downtime to decompress.

And from what I've seen, there is very, very little downtime when you have a kid. I love my nieces and nephews, but a little time with them goes a long way. My favorite part of visiting them is leaving again.

"I don't want kids," I say again, this time just above a whisper. Letting out a choked off laugh, I look at Amelia like, I'm seeing her for the first time. "I don't want kids."

"Great. You don't want kids," she says.

"Do you want kids?"

"That's none of your business." Her tone is light, but the tension in her shoulders tells me there's more to the story.

"Amelia."

She shakes her head. "I can't talk about this with you."

"Why?"

"Because it's blurry." She snaps off her gloves. "You're here on my table. I can't talk to you about my personal life, when I have to be professional. The lines are getting fuzzy, and I can't do fuzzy. I need crystal clear boundaries."

Navigating to a seated position, I'm almost at eye level with her.

"It's me. We're the only ones here. You can talk to me."

She sighs, shaking her head. "I can't."

Reaching for her, I grab her hand, pulling her into the V between my legs. My hands settle on her hips, light enough that she can break free, if she wants to.

I don't want her to.

"We can't," she breathes.

"Can't what?"

"This is a bad idea."

"What is?"

Amelia fists my T-shirt, pulling me to her and crashing our mouths together. Her lips are soft and yielding beneath mine, and as I lick into her mouth, something settles deep in my chest. Like something clicking into place. I didn't realize I was missing it until now, but holy fuck, does it feel *good*.

Cupping the back of her neck, the heel of my hand rests against the side of her throat. She shivers, but doesn't break the kiss. I slide my hand down until I'm cupping her throat instead. I don't exert pressure or try to choke her. That isn't my kink.

She moans into the kiss, her own hand mirroring the position on my throat. A heady dose of *want* courses through me, my cock pulsing in my athletic shorts. It's a vulnerable position, her hand on my throat. She could crush me. Choke me. She could do anything she wanted. She could destroy me.

I huff a laugh. She could destroy me even without her hand on my throat. She already owns me.

She pulls back, a furrow between her brows. "Something funny?"

Shaking my head, I reach for her again, but she steps out of my arms. "Just a thought."

"No," she finally says.

"No?" I lost track of what we were talking about.

"I don't want kids. My career comes first. This isn't a job I can balance a family with. It wouldn't be fair to them." She shrugs. "We all make sacrifices. I love Ainsley, and I'll love whatever other kids I give my brothers, but I don't want them for myself."

"You'll do it again? Be a surrogate?"

"I didn't hate being pregnant. And I'd do anything for Ty. They don't want a full clubhouse of kids, maybe one or two more." Her lips press into a thin line, and then she adds, "My career is more important to me."

"Hey, I get it. My career is important to me, too."

"So, you don't think it's a moral failing that I don't want to be a mother?" Amelia crosses her arms over her chest, staring me down.

"I think it's incredible that you made that decision for yourself and didn't let anyone influence you otherwise. Women are inundated with messages that they need to have kids to be complete. It's bullshit."

Her eyebrows go up.

"You are already a complete person, whether or not you have kids or a romantic partner. If you depend on other people for validation, what happens when they inevitably leave or die or move on?" I shake my head. "There's a difference between a partnership and a parasitic relationship, and not enough people recognize when something that used to be good turns into something bad."

Amelia swallows. "Your ex-wife?"

I lift a shoulder. "Her entire life was being a WAG. It wasn't about me. It was what I could do for her. And I didn't realize until I was in too deep, and by that point, I didn't see a way out."

"What was the final straw? If you don't mind me asking."

"She cheated. Said I wasn't around enough."

Scoffing, she rolls her eyes. "Yeah, because you're a professional hockey player. Travel goes with the territory."

"Yeah, well…" I shrug again. "It's over, and I'm moving on."

"Do you still talk to her?"

"Nope. Not since the divorce was finalized. And most of that process was through our lawyers."

Luckily, my agent insisted on a prenup all those years ago, so it was easy to divide assets. Aside from the final determination before the judge, I barely saw Harper after she served me with the papers.

Amelia hums.

"If you have any questions about the divorce or about my marriage, I'll answer them," I tell her. "I'm an open book."

She arches an eyebrow. "Do you go around telling all of your physical therapists your dirty laundry?"

"Nope. Just you."

Her cheeks flush.

"And by the way, when we get back to Boston, I'll have them reassign my case."

I've just decided this. It's the only way it'll work.

"Reassign?"

"I don't want to work with you anymore."

Flinching, she tries to turn away. "Okay."

"I don't want to work with you, because I want to do other things with you. And you said you can't do those things if we work together." My hands are still on her hips, and I squeeze lightly. "If we're on the road and nobody's available, I might need help with my knee, but whenever possible, I'll check in with Graham and Zac. I won't put you in an awkward position."

She unfurls from her tight ball of tension. "Oh?"

"Other positions are fair game." I give her a wolfish grin, and when she finally thaws, I grin for real. "I want to pursue something with you. You need clear boundaries at work. I'd be a dick, if I tried to steamroll over them."

"Yeah, you would," Amelia says. She winds her arms around my neck, stepping closer. "You want to pursue something with me?"

"I want to be with you." Laying my cards on the table, I say, "I want something real. And I think we can have that."

"What about your ex?"

"What about her?" I don't see what Harper has to do with this.

"Don't you miss her?"

I shake my head. "To be honest, I was emotionally checked out for a good two years before it ended. I didn't have the courage to say anything. I thought all marriages were unhappy, and that it was just a part of life."

She hums, her eyes roving over my face.

"But seeing Tyler and Brandon, seeing Larsson and Vanessa… They give me hope."

"Hope?"

"Maybe someday, I can find that." I shake my head. "But that's too much pressure to put on a new relationship, so forget I said anything."

"Oh? We're in a relationship now?" Her eyebrows arch up, a smirk on her face.

"I'd like to be."

All the remaining tension in her body releases, and she leans into me. "Me, too."

twenty-two

. . .

Amelia

BEING in a secret relationship with someone you work with is surprisingly difficult. Jason is around all the time. Every time I turn around, he's watching me. In the lounge, in the equipment bay, in the medical suites. And as it turns out... I like being watched. Even if my clothes are on.

True to his word, he's been seeking out Zac and Graham to work on his knee. I haven't had to deal with him in a professional capacity since that day in Ottawa.

On the road, we're careful to keep our distance, but when we're in Boston, I spend the night at his place. We keep the blinds closed, thank you very much.

Ty and Brandon guessed I'm seeing someone, but they haven't asked, so I haven't told them any lies. Jason and I agreed that nobody can find out about us. Not yet. Not while we're still so new.

Technically, there are ways around the non-fraternization policy—Sven and Vanessa are proof—but I'm not ready to officially declare our fledgling relationship for public gossip. And if there's one thing I learned about hockey players, it's that they love to gossip.

Which makes it difficult to spend any time together,

because other players are always dropping by Jason's apartment to chat or hang out.

The first time he asked me to hide in his bedroom, I was pissed. But the more I thought about it, if someone found me in his place, it would only invite questions I don't want to answer. I don't want to outright *lie*. But I don't want to volunteer the information, either.

But tonight—it's just for us.

He ordered dinner from my favorite restaurant, opened a bottle of wine, and lit some candles. Under the table, his feet tangle with mine as we eat our chicken Marsala and chat about our day. Snow is falling, and up here on the nineteenth floor, it's the perfect date night in.

Until someone bangs on the door.

Jason sighs, looking at me with regret on his face. "Do you mind?"

Truthfully, I do mind. But not enough to force the issue. Not with the potential of losing my job hanging over my head.

I escape to the bedroom, closing the door behind me.

"What is it?" I hear Jason say, a hint of steel in his voice. "This isn't a good time."

"What's up with you?" Logan says. "Oh, shit. Are you on a date?"

"Shut up," Jason says. "What's going on?"

"Who is she?"

"Not talking about it." There's a growl in his tone that would stop a grizzly bear in its tracks.

But Logan isn't a grizzly bear. He's an oblivious hockey player.

"I didn't know you were seeing anyone."

"It's new," Jason clips out. "Why are you here?"

Logan sighs. "You said… you said I could talk to you. But—"

My boyfriend sighs. "Okay. Lay it on me."

"Nah. You have company. I'll just… I don't know. Wallow in my misery."

With anyone else, it would be a cutting barb, but Logan isn't being snarky; he genuinely means it.

"Talk to MacGregor," Jason says. "Maybe he'll…"

"Punch me in the face, and then ask to be traded to keep his sister safe from me?" Logan's laugh is hollow. "Yeah, no thanks."

"He can't throw a punch."

Logan laughs outright. "Yeah, because that's the part we're focusing on."

"It might not be that bad."

"I can't risk it."

"So, you'd rather be alone and miserable than happy with her?"

"I don't want to jeopardize the relationship with my best friend. Not when it impacts the team, too."

"The team will be fine."

"But do you *know* that? If he punches me in the face, Coach will bench him. Hell, probably me, too."

"So, don't let him punch you," Jason says.

Logan chuckles. "Yeah, because it's that easy. Hey, I'm in love with your little sister, and have been for ten years. Let's go hit the weights. Fuck, he'd probably drop them on me on purpose."

"Shit, man. Ten years?"

"I told you. She's the only one I've ever wanted."

"I did some research."

"Oh?"

"On being demisexual. I'm honored you told me." Jason pauses, as if realizing he just outed Logan to me. "We won't tell anyone."

Logan groans. "She's in the bedroom, isn't she?"

My face heats. He can't see me. There's no way he knows it's *me*, just an anonymous woman in the apartment.

"Who?"

"Whoever you're seeing."

"Yeah. But she won't say anything."

He pauses. "You aren't seeing Hailey, right?"

Jason laughs, the sound warming me through. "No. You have her all to yourself."

Logan groans again, like he's in pain. "Yeah, if I can ever get out of my own way."

"You will." There's a clapping sound, like maybe he smacked his teammate's shoulder. "But for now, I need you to get out of my way."

"Yeah, yeah. Enjoy your date."

"Seriously, man. Are we good?" Jason asks.

"Yeah. I needed to talk about it."

"I'm here for you anytime. Just… maybe send me a text first."

Logan chuckles. "Yeah. Sounds good."

The door opens and closes, and then footsteps approach. Jason opens the bedroom door, an apologetic look on his face.

"I'm sorry," he says. "I shouldn't have asked you to—"

"You should have," I tell him. "It's fine. I know the deal. Until we're ready to go public, this is for the best."

He collapses onto the bed beside me. "Yeah, but it makes me feel shitty. Like I'm keeping you my dirty little secret."

"I mean, technically…"

Lifting his head, he stares at me.

Laughing, I run my hand through his hair. "But it doesn't bother me. Not when the alternative makes me break out in hives."

He arches a brow. "Hives, huh? I don't see any hives."

"Better look closer, then."

Rolling my body under his, he dips his head to kiss me. Every time he kisses me, it's like fireworks going off deep in my belly.

Last night, he went to the bar with some of the guys, and I

went to dinner with Ty and Brandon. I haven't spent as much time with them lately. It was the first night Jason and I spent apart in Boston in the two and a half weeks we've been together. I missed his stupid face, going to bed with him beside me, and waking up snuggled next to him.

So instead, I waited until he got home, stripped naked, and gave him a show. For old time's sake.

Except this time, he called me, and I heard the noises he made while he jacked himself off, the groans I'd love to swallow down. The same way I've swallowed *other* things down.

Now, his hard cock digs into my hip, but he makes no move to get me naked. He seems satisfied to make out, kissing simply for the sake of kissing. It doesn't always have to be a race to see who can get naked first. It's simply how it usually turns out.

It's been a long time since I indulged in a man's company. When I was pregnant, I didn't want anyone to touch me, and before that, I was on such intense hormones preparing for the IVF, transfer, and the first twelve weeks... I didn't want to risk any accidents.

Colorado was lonely. This career isn't for the faint of heart, and after a while, the travel got to me. I didn't have the strong friendships there that I've found now. I didn't have any allies who would spend time with me. Whenever the team flew in to a new city, I found a guy in a bar or an app, but it was all so... impersonal. Get right down to business and then get out, never hearing from them again.

I missed having a connection. I missed wanting a connection.

But with Jason... I have one. Our connection goes beyond our bedroom activities. I *enjoy* spending time with him, talking about our days, dissecting the latest team gossip. I like *him*.

Maybe we're rushing into things, spending so much time together. It must be the honeymoon period, right?

He's only been divorced for a few months. But I'm not looking for a ring. I'm not even looking for a future. All I'm thinking about is right now, and how perfect this is. Would it be nice if the team knew? Sure, it would. Would it be nice to not have to worry about my job? Yes, definitely.

But if it risks this fragile new relationship, I'd rather keep it quiet until we're more settled. Jason means too much to me to risk telling anyone.

I don't want to give him up. Not now, maybe not ever.

twenty-three

. . .

Jason

SEATTLE IS KICKING OUR ASSES. Who would expect the last place team in the league to find the mettle to absolutely obliterate the second place team? It's our first game back after the All Star break, and we are rusty as fuck.

Boston is at the top of the standings in the Eastern conference, second only to Colorado in the Western conference. We're absolutely killing it. The team is gelling like never before, half the team is on a points streak, and MacGregor scored two hat tricks in the last five games.

We're on fire. Just not tonight.

I'm playing like I'm twenty-seven again, and not thirty-seven. Getting regular athletic massages is definitely helping, even if I can't get them from Amelia. I respect her too much to put her job in jeopardy, and in the bedroom, we're careful to keep work and my knee issues separate from us.

As much as I love hockey and playing the game I love, the travel is starting to get to me. I've done this for more than a third of my life, and had a good little wife waiting at home for me, but I never itched to get back to her the way I do with Amelia. When we're on the road, I can't talk to her, can't touch her, and can't fall asleep holding her.

I have to keep my distance. I can't be the reason anyone finds out about us. Not before she's ready.

If it was solely up to me, I'd scream it out from the rooftops. I'd tell management, my teammates, her brothers… everyone.

But I would never push her to announce it before she's ready. However long it takes, I'll bide my time. The ball is in her court.

Unlike the puck, which is decidedly in the Boston defensive zone. I shake my head and try to focus on the game in front of me. One of the opposing players shoots, but Henry deflects it, dumping it out of his glove.

Another player tries for a rebound, but Sinclair gets a stick on it and finally manages to clear the puck to Seattle's end. Coach slaps my shoulder, and I vault over the boards and onto the ice.

We're down 4-1 with seven minutes to go. It's an impossible task they're asking of us. There's no way we can do it.

Larsson and I flank MacGregor as we zoom into the Seattle zone. He passes to me, and I kick it back to Larsson. He pauses for a second, faking like he's about to shoot, and then saucers the puck over to MacGregor.

The center's one-timer is brutal, and as he slaps the puck on goal, my knee buckles.

I'm not doing anything strenuous. My stick is on the ice, ready for action, but Joseph, the Seattle defenseman guarding me, isn't touching me. Nothing *happens*.

But my knee can't support me, and I go down. The wind is knocked out of me, and I sprawl on the ice, trying to figure out what the fuck just happened.

"What the fuck," Joseph shouts. "I didn't even touch you."

The goal horn sounds. MacGregor's snipe was successful.

It takes considerable effort to get back up onto my feet. I'm still laboring as I join my teammates for the post-goal celly.

"What happened?" Larsson mutters in our huddle at center ice.

"Just tripped."

"Mmhmm. Your knee?"

I shake my head. "I'm fine."

We skate past the bench to bump knuckles with the rest of the team, and Derek pulls me in.

"Let's talk," he says. It's not a request; it's an order.

"I'm fine," I say again.

"He didn't trip you." He says it like an accusation.

Grabbing a water bottle, I take a drink, and then spray my face and the back of my neck. "My knee is acting up. I'm fine."

"I heard you the first time," Derek snaps. "Does it hurt?"

"Not any more than usual."

That's the honest truth; it always hurts. No matter how warm and stretched I am before a game, after three hours of activity, it always aches. The osteoarthritis is something I'll have to live with for the rest of my life.

There are invasive procedures, but they have side effects, and it would mean the end of my playing career. At thirty-seven, it's doubtful I'd come back from it. And being in the last year of my contract, it's unlikely any other team would want me after surgery.

There's still a chance the Grizzlies will want me for another two years. That's my Plan A, at least. But it means keeping healthy, doing all of my PT, and not letting the bumps and bruises get to me.

Easton, Jenkins, and Gonzo are on the ice, and I try to focus, but the throbbing in my knee makes it hard to concentrate on the instructions Coach yells in my ear. They rotate off, the third line taking the ice, and I start to shake, anticipating. I love hockey. I *love* it with every fiber of my being. What will I do when it's not part of my life anymore? I don't think I'll be able to stand it.

Coach claps my shoulder, and then I'm heaving myself over the boards again, right when Logan gets control of the puck. There's nobody in the Seattle defensive end.

I put on a burst of speed, hurtling myself forward to be in the right place, and the puck lands on my tape with precision accuracy.

There's no time to set up a play. I fire at the goaltender, the puck clanging off the post on its way to the back of the net. Quick and dirty, just the way I like it.

My knee fucking *throbs* from the exertion. I do my best not to limp off the ice, but the tightness on Derek's face tells me I'm in for a world of trouble.

———

An hour later, after cooling down and showering, I'm in the PT bay, where Derek digs his fingers into my knee.

"I'm fine," I say, for the tenth time.

"Shut up," he snaps.

"It works. I can play."

"I didn't say you can't. I said, you'll to hurt yourself worse than you already have." He sighs. "It's nothing structural. Ice. Elevate. Rest. The usual."

"Yes, sir," I say, with a sarcastic salute.

The athletic trainer glares at me. "Go on, get out of here. Don't do anything stupid."

He wraps my knee with ice, and I return to the dressing room. When I finally have a chance to check my phone, there's a text from Amelia.

How are you feeling?

I don't lie to her.

I've been better.

I'm sorry. This sucks.

And I know she's talking about more than simply not being able to interact.

Miss you.

I text back, before shoving the phone into my pocket.

I can't look at her, because if anyone takes one glance at my face while I do, this whole charade is over. I can't talk to her without it turning flirty; I can't touch her without pulling her into my arms.

I miss her so fucking much, and she's only in the next room.

The team bus delivers us to the airfield, and as we board the plane, I take my usual spot in the middle, aisle seat. She's a few rows ahead of me on the right side, sitting with Patrice, so it's the perfect location to covertly watch her.

Gonzo drops into the seat beside me. "How's the knee?"

"It's fine."

I barely want to get into it with Derek, much less anyone else.

He sighs. "Yeah. Sure."

"Everything okay with you?"

He opens his mouth, and then closes it. "Yeah. I'm fine."

"Uh-huh. You know, you can talk to me."

"Yep." There's a note of finality in his tone. "I just want to sit here and sleep, so you just go back to staring at Amelia, and I'll—"

My jaw drops. "I'm not—"

He snorts. "Please. You totally have a thing for her."

"I—"

"Don't worry, I won't tell anyone," he says. "I think she likes you, too. I always see her smiling at you."

Shit, neither of us are as discreet as we think we are. Guess her idea of keeping our relationship under wraps is a good one.

"She smiles at a lot of people," I say, with no conviction.

"Yeah, but not the way she smiles at you." Gonzo shrugs. "Ask her out. See what happens."

I let out a soft hum. "Maybe."

"The team wouldn't have an issue with it. We all like her."

I like her, too. That's kind of the problem.

"I'll think about it," I finally say, shutting it down.

Gonzo passes out as soon as we're in the air, but I can't sleep. All I can think about is what would happen if anyone found out about us. What do I say? I can't deny it. I can't lie.

We land in Dallas at six o'clock in the morning with the time change, and the bus gets us to the team hotel in short order. My entire body aches when Vanessa hands me a key, and I make my way to the room.

But once I get to there and change into comfortable clothes, I'm wide awake. Pulling out my phone, I text Amelia.

I need to see you.

She doesn't fight me. She doesn't say we can't. All she texts back is a number—a room number.

I'm outside her door less than five minutes later. It's like I was struck by a live wire, every nerve ending flayed by the electrical current running through me. I knock lightly on the door, my knuckles still on the wood when it opens.

Amelia fists her hand in my T-shirt, and pulls me bodily into the room.

"Hi," I whisper. I'm not sure why I'm whispering. There's nobody in the room except for us.

"This is a bad idea," she says, before she kisses me.

It's the first time we've kissed in four days. I'm aching for her, my entire body reacting, but I tamp down my baser urges. I haven't held or touched her in four long days. I'm going to savor this.

I break the kiss to yawn.

"Come on, let's sleep," she says.

Grumbling under my breath, I pretend to be put out, but as soon as she draws back the covers and slides in, I scoot in beside her and fold my arms around her.

Amelia presses lightly on my shoulder, and I roll over until my back is to her. She contorts her body around mine, wrapping me in her embrace. Everything in me says I shouldn't like being the little spoon as much as I do, but I don't need to listen to toxic hypermasculinity bullshit.

When she holds me, everything is okay with the world. Sure, my body is still battered and bruised from the game. Everything hurts. But I can get through—because I have her. She makes everything better.

And as I drift off to sleep, I wish that I could do this every night: fall asleep beside the woman I love.

twenty-four

. . .

Amelia

JASON IS GONE when I wake up, the only evidence he was here a hastily scribbled note on the hotel stationary.

Last night was risky. It can't happen again.

We have the day off, so even though breakfast is optional in the team room, I take myself out to a nearby diner with my Kindle. I would kill for some migas right about now.

Except it seems the team had the same idea, because half the players are seated at a table near the window.

"Amelia!" Sinclair says. "Sit with us!"

"Oh, I couldn't—"

"Come on, we don't bite," Jenkins says, waggling his eyebrows. "Unless you ask us to, that is."

Despite myself, I laugh, and I allow the waitress to pull a chair over. So, my quiet morning to myself turns into breakfast with seven hockey players, two assistant coaches, and the statistical analyst. I'm the only woman, but I don't feel unsafe or unwelcome; if anything, I finally feel like I *belong*.

Halfway through the meal, MacGregor, Logan, and Gonzo enter the restaurant, Jason on their heels. His eyebrows go up when he sees me sitting with his teammates, but he doesn't otherwise react.

They're seated at another table on the opposite side of the diner. My phone buzzes in my pocket, but I don't dare pull it out, not when the other guys can see the screen.

Excusing myself to the restroom, I duck into the stall and check my phone, half-expecting the worst.

But there's no jealous rant from Jason. There's only a quick message: *Sorry to sneak out this morning. Miss you already. Have a good day off.*

I should give him more credit. He's a grown man, not an immature fuckboy. He knows where we stand.

As much as I want to go by their table to say hi, it's not a good idea. So, after washing my hands, I return to my meal. Sinclair, Reynolds, and Jenkins keep me laughing with more and more outlandish jokes, feeding off each other's intensity. It's all harmless fun.

Easton pays for the meal—he pays for everyone, despite my insistence I can cover my own food—and I walk back to the hotel with Jenkins and Sinclair. It's in the low fifties, a welcome respite from the frigid temperatures of the Northeast in late February, but it's still not exactly pool weather.

Luckily, this hotel has an indoor pool.

After a quick change into my suit, I head for the pool, intending to get some laps in. I don't mind other form of exercise, but swimming is my favorite. There's something peaceful about the weightlessness of the water.

Nobody else is around while I do my laps for the better part of an hour. I'm almost done when a person gets into the pool on the other end. I do two more laps before popping up over the side wall, breathing hard.

The man in the lane beside me is an impressive figure cutting through the water, the muscles in his big, broad back flexing with every movement. I appreciate his athleticism. He's strong and in great shape.

But I have no interest in him, aside from academic fascination. When I was in grad school, I worked with a few members of the university's swim team.

Shaking my head, I pull myself from the water. I dry my hands and face with a towel, and then pick up my Kindle and water bottle, bringing them to the hot tub at the other end of the cavernous room. The hot water is amazing on my sore and jet-lagged body. I don't even need the jets; the heat is enough to relax me.

Lost in my book, I hardly notice when another body joins me in the hot tub. Forcing myself to look up, I nod at the person—and then I freeze.

Because Jason sits across from me, his muscular arms spread across the cement ring on the outside of the tub. The water line hits him directly on the solar plexus, highlighting the curve of his pecs and his strong shoulders.

"Hey, stranger," he says, giving me a teasing grin.

"What are you doing here?"

His grin curves into a self-satisfied smirk. "You mean you didn't notice me doing laps?"

I swallow. "I didn't realize it was you." I have no interest in checking out any man other than mine.

Shaking his head, he huffs out a laugh. "Only you, babe."

My eyes widen, and I look frantically around the pool. But we're the only two here.

"Derek said to do my cardio in the water. Doesn't want me tweaking the knee more."

I frown. "It's bad?"

"Well, it's not good." His massive shoulders lift in a shrug. "I'll get through it."

"I could—"

Jason shakes his head. "Let's not worry about it right now. Tell me about your day yesterday."

Laughing, I roll my eyes. "I worked. You saw me."

"Yeah, but I didn't *see* you. How were your sessions? Anyone out of line?"

"The team is great. Everything went well."

He studies me, his brown eyes intent on my face. "You have plans for tonight?"

"Robby, Joaquin, Patrice, and I are going to the movies. There's a new James Bond flick out."

Sven and Vanessa are having a date night. They're so cute together, but I can't deny how jealous I am every time they eat breakfast together in the meal room, or sit beside each other on the plane.

I want that with Jason. I want that for us.

"Hm, I've heard of it. Maybe the guys and I will go."

"I can't stop you. But it's our thing. You don't need to crash it."

"I know. I just want to spend time with you." His face softens. "I hate that we can't."

"Me, too."

Every day that goes by, it's harder to remember my reasons for keeping our relationship quiet. But then, my paycheck lands in my bank account, and I remember. I'm incredibly fortunate that Brandon and Tyler gave me a place to land when I was let go from Colorado, but if it happens again with the Grizzlies… I'd probably have to leave Boston. I've already applied to all the major sports organizations. Sure, there are a bunch of universities I could try, and I suppose I could always go the clinical route…

But that's not what I love. I want to work with hockey players, as boneheaded as they may be. It's what I want to spend my life doing.

Besides, Jason's contract is up at the end of the season. He could sign with another team—or worse, be traded. Who knows where he'll be? He says he wants to stay in Boston, but it's not necessarily up to him. If the team needs to move him, he could be *heavily encouraged* to waive his no-trade clause.

On top of that, it's incredibly early in our relationship to make long-term plans. We've only been together for a month, and nobody knows about us. He just ended a marriage. It's too soon to think about a future, too soon to change my life plans.

Jason reaches across the hot tub, and since nobody else is around, I let him pull me across the small pool and into his arms. I straddle him on the stone bench, my arms winding around his neck.

"Hi," he whispers, his eyes darting between my lips and my breasts.

My swimsuit is a terribly unsexy one-piece that smashes my boobs into pancakes. It's designed more for athletics than aesthetics. There's a cutout where the straps crisscross on my back, and that's where his fingers go, sliding along the strip of exposed skin.

"Hi," I whisper back, feeling self-conscious and silly.

He arches up, his lips meeting mine in a heady kiss. I thought the fire would die down as we got used to each other, but if anything, it's only growing hotter as we learn each other.

His strong body feels so good beneath me, and as he grows hard against my ass, I can't resist rocking against him. Even with the water and the fabric of our swimsuits between us, he feels amazing between my legs.

"Hey, now," he murmurs. "None of that."

"Why not?"

He kisses my neck, the soft scrape of his stubble sending my pulse skyrocketing. I dig my fingers into his shoulders, massaging some of the tension.

"Don't start something you won't finish," Jason warns.

"Who said I'm not going to finish?" Grinding onto him, I swivel my hips, and the groan he lets out is satisfaction to my ears.

My hands trace over his sculpted body, touching him both above and under the water. He feels as incredible as ever. I grow slick between my legs, and it has nothing to do with the hot tub.

There's a snap that echoes through the pool, and then footsteps, and I break apart from Jason. Breathing hard, I move to the other side of the hot tub, trying to act like nothing is going on.

My core throbs with want, my nipples tight buds. I'm panting, attempting to regulate my breathing.

There are more footsteps, followed by a shriek of laughter. Looking over my shoulder, I see a woman with two boys. Preteens, maybe.

One boy strips off his shirt and shoes, and then cannonballs into the pool. The other boy—his brother?—shakes his head and enters the pool more sedately using the ladder.

Mood? Killed.

Jason catches my hand. "Let's get out of here," he murmurs.

Need courses through me, and despite my misgivings, I give in to my impulsive side. "Your place or mine?"

twenty-five

. . .

Jason

IT'S clear from the get-go that Dallas has our number. It's the middle of the second period, and we're tied at 0-0. The day off was much needed, but I'm moving slow as molasses.

Though, finally getting to be with Amelia after four days apart? Worth it.

After we fucked the horniness into abeyance, we curled up in each other's arms and dozed. It was so nice to simply hold her again. I already miss her, and she's just a few feet away off the ice, watching me from the tunnel.

I shake my head, trying to focus. I can't afford any more distractions.

She snuck out of my room a little past four, and then got ready for dinner and a movie with her friends. As much as I wanted to join them, I forced myself to spend time with MacGregor, Logan, and Gonzo instead. After dinner, we went back to MacGregor's room and played video games. It was the perfect low-key night to cap off a great day. But it would have been better if Amelia was there with me.

No. Focus.

Coach calls for a line change, and I vault over the boards, flanked by Larsson and MacGregor. We set up shop in

Dallas's end, and as anticipation wars with adrenaline in my veins, a steady sense of calm rushes over me.

This is where I belong. This is what I'm meant to do. No matter what it takes, I'll work as hard as required to stay in this league. Nothing else compares. Nothing I'll ever do for the rest of my life will ever be as meaningful as this.

Although it's is a low-scoring game, it's as high intensity as ever. Dallas's players are huge, and their hits are massive. I spin to avoid a check from number 72, rubbernecking with the boards to escape. I don't even have the puck on my stick.

But Allen and I go way back; he's had it out for me ever since we both played for Detroit seven years ago, and I got more ice time than he did. The back and forth proved was good for both of us; it made us better players. Doesn't keep him from hating me, though.

I learned to let it go. I don't hold grudges. Hockey is too volatile a sport. Sometimes, I'm bitter about the plays that injured me, the hit that caused my third knee surgery, the trip that broke my wrist in the playoffs. But it comes in waves; it's not a steady-state thing. Mainly, it's when it twinges that I get salty.

Right now, I'm healthy as a horse. After the athletic massage Graham did on my knee this morning, I feel better than ever. Spending time with Amelia definitely helped, too. Now, we only need to figure out a way to hook up on every road trip.

MacGregor passes the puck, and I scramble to meet it, and it lands on my tape with a satisfying *thwack*. I carry it up the center of the ice, deking around Allen and Haney, the massive defenseman.

Larsson is behind me, and I drop the puck back to him, turning to meet Allen's check.

And that's when I hear it. A pop.

White-hot pain laces through me, and I collapse onto the

ice. Tears well in my eyes, and I blink a few times, trying to breathe through the pain.

The refs realize I'm still on the ice, and call the play dead. My heartbeat echoes loudly in my ears when I try to sit up. I get halfway there before the pain gets to be too much and I have to stop.

Larsson skids to a stop, inadvertently spraying me with ice. "What is it? Your knee?"

I shake my head. It's not my knee that's hurting. "I don't know."

"Derek's on his way," MacGregor reports.

Around me, all the players take a knee. It's never a good thing when a guy goes down; it's worse when he doesn't get back up.

Derek scurries over, wearing grippy cleats over his shoes. "Your knee?"

"I heard a pop," I tell him. I'm sweating, and it has nothing to do with the game. "Something is wrong."

"You need a stretcher? You didn't hit your head." He studies me carefully, assessing my condition. "Do we need to go into concussion protocol?"

I shake my head again. "It's my ankle. Or my leg. I don't know. I can't get up on my own."

"Okay. We'll do it together." Derek nods to MacGregor and Larsson, and my teammates grip my arms and lift me onto my skates.

I try to put weight on my left leg, and pain radiates through me. Blinking back the water in my eyes, I swallow and try to skate with my left foot hovering off the ice.

There's a cheer, and then applause, and I realize it's for me. Stick taps on the boards. For standing up. For doing the bare fucking minimum to get my bearings back.

"You've got this, Cap," MacGregor says, clapping my shoulder. "You'll be right as rain tomorrow."

"Nothing a bit of PT can't fix," Larsson adds.

I choke out a laugh. "Sure. Yeah."

We stumble-glide to the chute, and then Derek helps me keep the weight off my leg as we hobble down the chute.

"Amelia," he barks. "You're my eyes and ears."

She salutes him, but there's no disguising the worry on her face. "You got it, boss."

It's almost good that she can't be here for this part; I don't want her to see me like this.

Inside the dressing room, Derek heads straight to the medical bay. He hoists me onto the table, and then takes a pair of scissors to my laces, slicing through them. He eases my skate off my foot.

"Oh, *fuck*." Without the skate compressing everything, the pain is worse.

He takes off my second skate—probably so he won't get sliced by accident—and then cuts through my socks and tears off my shin guards until my left leg is bare to the chill of the room. But I'm burning up.

There's a knock on the open door, and then Doc Hudson is bustling into the office. He's wearing a team polo and warmup jacket rather than a white coat, but there's no mistaking his authority.

I lay back on the table as he does a visual examination while Derek debriefs him, and then he snaps on a pair of gloves and examines me himself. Every touch hurts more than the one before, and I can't keep my mouth shut.

Luckily, Doc is used to a little cursing.

"We'll need an MRI to be sure," he finally says, reaching for the tablet that Derek hands him. "Looks to be your Achilles."

"Fuck." I cover my face with my hands. "Do I need surgery?"

"Probably." At least he's honest about it. "You'll be out for a bit."

"The rest of the season?" There's only seven weeks left before playoffs start.

"Most likely," Doc says. "I'll call the ambulance."

"No. I don't—"

"We need to do an MRI, and we can't do it here, son. I'll stay with you the whole time."

"Is there anyone we can call?" Derek asks. "A girlfriend?"

I shake my head. "I need my phone."

"Harper?" Doc asks. *Guess he didn't hear about the divorce.*

"No. Someone else."

Derek raises his brows. "You're seeing someone?"

There's commotion in the hall behind us as the team funnels into the dressing room for intermission.

"It's new," I clip out, trying to swing my leg over the side of the table.

"Whoa. Where do you think you're going?" Doc sets a hand on my chest.

"To see my team. They have to know I'm okay. They need a pep talk."

I know what it's like to see a guy go down on the ice—and when he doesn't get back up.

It's my job to lead this team. To inspire them, to boost them up, and to give them a dose of reality when needed. I didn't want it to happen like this, though.

Derek helps me hobble out of the exam room, and into the visiting dressing room. The guys are assembled at their cubbies, half of them undressed. I don't like to take off my kit between periods, but other guys exchange their jerseys or pads for fresh ones.

A silence falls over the room as I limp out, and then stuttered applause floods the room.

"I'll be okay," I tell them, leaning against the wall for support. "I'm going to get checked out, but I'll be alright. You guys are going to score a fucking goal, you're going to win the damn game, and when you get back to Boston in three days, I'll be there to cheer you on."

Logan frowns. "You think you're out?"

"Still need to run some tests, but I don't think I'll be back on the ice for the next game, maybe two." That's all I'll say about it.

My gaze roves over my teammates, my brothers, and the staff members who support us in everything we do.

And then I catch sight of Amelia in the corner. Her eyes are glassy, but they won't meet mine.

"I'll be okay," I say, my gaze focused on her. "Now, go kick some Dallas ass."

twenty-six

. . .

Amelia

THERE'S a protocol for these situations. One of the team's medical staff has to stay back to monitor and accompany any injured player. Dr. Hudson has privileges at the local hospital, but it isn't his job to babysit during the trip home or the recovery.

So, when Derek calls Graham and me into his office Jason's speech, I already know what he's going to say.

"I'll do it," I volunteer. "I'll stay with—McKittrick." *Shit, I almost called him Jason in front of my boss.*

Derek eyes me. "You sure?"

"We're neighbors. My brother delivers his meals, so I have access to his apartment. I'll get him back home and situated."

Not to mention, I'd drive myself nuts with worry, if he was alone—or worse, with Graham.

"Thanks, Amelia," Derek finally says. "Doc wants to get an MRI, but he thinks McKittrick needs surgery, so it might be a day or two before he's cleared to fly."

"Got it. I have it covered," I say. There's nobody on my roster who Graham can't handle, especially for a day or two. After all, there's a reason two PTs travel with the team.

My boss nods at me. "We'll handle the rest of the game. Touch base with Vanessa on the protocol."

Dismissed, I exit the medical bay, and seek out Vanessa, who handles all the logistics. She's sequestered in an office, typing quickly on her laptop. She looks up when I knock on the doorframe, a backpack already slung across my shoulders.

"I booked a hotel room for each of you tonight, although you probably won't need them," she says.

Blowing out a breath, the realization sits heavy in my belly. "Because you think he needs surgery."

"Just covering my bases," Van says. "Call me or text the results of the MRI. Once he's cleared to fly, I'll coordinate the charter."

"It might be a few days, if he needs surgery."

"We'll take it one day at a time. I already have Robby pulling both your suitcases from the bus, and they'll be delivered to your hotel rooms." She sighs. "This sucks. It never gets easier."

"He'll be okay." I don't know if I'm trying to reassure her or myself. "He has to be."

She hands me a sheaf of papers. Insurance information, injury protocol, hotel reservations… everything I need is in this packet. I stuff it into my backpack.

Vanessa's phone buzzes, and she checks the screen. "Okay. Your car is here. The hospital is four miles away."

Giving her a nod, I head for the tunnels, jogging to the gate. Security nods at me when I pass by, a team badge swinging from my neck.

The drive to the hospital takes for-fucking-ever. Finally, we pull into the emergency room, and I hurry to the reception desk.

"I'm with the Boston Grizzlies. I'm here for Jason McKittrick." I show her my team badge and employee ID. "Dr. Hudson is expecting me."

The nurse hums, not looking impressed. "Who's that?"

"He's your VIP patient. He was probably rushed straight for an MRI." I hold up my employee ID. "I'm his patient advocate. I'll fill out his insurance information, but first I need to see him."

She finally nods, handing over a visitor's badge. "Second floor."

"Thank you!" I take the badge and jog down the hallway.

The nurses at the second station are moderately more helpful. Jason is in for the MRI now, and Dr. Hudson is outside the radiology booth, wearing hospital scrubs.

"Ah, Amelia," he says, with a wide smile. "I didn't think I'd see you here."

"Derek sent me."

His blue eyes twinkle. "Yes, I suppose he did."

"What do you need from me?"

"He'll be out in a little while, and then the radiologist and I will review the scans." Doc sighs. "If it's what I expect, he'll be wheeled upstairs for surgery."

"You'll do it tonight? He won't have to wait for swelling to go down?"

"I won't know until I see it again, but there appeared to be minimal swelling." He shakes his head. "Such a shame. It's probably the end of his career."

My stomach drops. "Are you sure?"

"He's thirty-seven. There are only six weeks left of the season. And he's in the last year of his contract."

"No team will want to touch him," I say slowly, putting the pieces together.

Fuck. Who will tell him? Will it be better or worse for it to come from me? Will he always blame me for delivering the news? Maybe it will be better to hear it from a neutral party…

Doc nods, remorse all over his face. "Such a shame to go out this way."

The door to radiology opens, and an orderly wheels Jason out in a chair.

"Now, I'll review the scans," Doc announces to both of us. "Hang out in the ER for a bit, and then we'll figure out where to go from there."

Jason nods, a muscle clenching in his jaw.

Shit. How much did he overhear?

"Right this way, ma'am," the orderly says, jerking his head. I fall into step beside him as he leads us down the hallway, into the elevator, and back to the ER. We're shown to a private room—reserved for VIP patients, no doubt—and finally, *finally*, we're alone.

Jason clears his throat. "Thank you for being here."

"There's nowhere else I'd rather be." Crossing the room, I reach for his hand, taking it in my own. "How are you doing?"

He scowls. "How do you think I'm doing?"

"Hey, I'm just asking," I say, with forced lightness. "Are you in pain? Do you need more meds?"

There's an IV attached to his left hand, a bag of saline slowly dripping into his system. He didn't shower after the game, so he smells a bit ripe, but it's nothing I can't deal with. I run my hand through his sweaty hair, pushing it off his face.

"You can talk to me."

"I can't, though," he bites out. "How do I know what you'll report back to Derek and Coach?"

It's my turn to scowl. "I won't tell them anything you don't want me to. I may be here as your patient advocate, but I only volunteered because it's *you*. I couldn't bear the thought of you being here by yourself—or worse, with Graham."

Jason's eyes soften. "I'm sorry. I'm not feeling great."

"I don't blame you. It's a lot to deal with." I cup his cheek. "I'm here for you. Whatever you need, babe."

Bending down, I kiss him lightly, trying to reassure him.

He squeezes my hand, so tight it almost hurts, when he kisses me back. It's as electric as ever, even if he's wearing a hospital gown. I just had him twelve hours ago, but it already feels like twelve years since the last time.

The door snicks open, and we snap apart. I hurry to the other side of the small room.

Dr. Hudson raises an eyebrow, but doesn't comment on my red face or Jason's labored breathing.

"Well, son," he says, and Jason blows out a breath.

"It's official?" Pain laces his voice.

"Achilles tendon rupture," Doc says. "We'll get you prepped for surgery. You're being admitted. It may be a couple of hours before we can get into the O.R."

"But it's happening tonight?" I ask.

He nods. "Before dawn, that's for sure. I'll be assisted by Dr. Iglesias. She's the best ortho doc in Dallas. She'll handle your aftercare while I meet the team in St. Louis. Two days, maybe three, and then we'll get you home."

"Thanks," Jason says tightly.

"Son, you stink. We'll have a nurse come by to give you a sponge bath," he adds. "Unless you'd rather do it yourself, Amelia?" He winks at me.

Crap. So, he definitely saw us. Will he tell the rest of the team? Will he tell management? Fuck, fuck, fuck.

I choke out a strained laugh. "A nurse should be fine. Thanks for offering."

Doc hums, clearly amused. "I'll see you in the operating room, Jason. Amelia, I'll find you after. Once we're in there, it shouldn't take more than an hour or two."

"Thanks, Doc."

He leaves us alone again, and I turn to Jason.

"What are you thinking?"

He blows out a breath. "I'm glad you're here," he says quietly. His rich brown eyes meet mine. "I'm glad it's you."

"I wish it wasn't you," I admit. "When you went down…"

It was one of the scariest moments of my life. He didn't get up. It took him a *long* time to get back up, and then when he limped off the ice? My heart was in my throat. I could hardly concentrate on the rest of the period, my only thought the man in front of me now.

Jason shakes his head. "We can't think about that." He reaches out his hand and I take it, his strong fingers curling around mine. "We just have to get through tonight."

"Are you worried? About the surgery?"

"Not any more than I was the last time." He sighs. "First time I've had an Achilles issue, though. Usually it's my knee that's being operated on."

"Is there anyone I can call for you?"

"I should probably tell my mother. She was blowing up my phone earlier." He looks around the room. "I don't even know where it is."

"I'll check in with the nurse. Do you need anything else?"

He reaches for me, drawing me close until I'm practically leaning on the cot he's lying on. "Don't go. Not now."

"I won't leave you," I promise.

twenty-seven

. . .

Jason

EVERYTHING IS HAZY. I don't like it.

Pain dances at the periphery of my mind, held back only by the strong drugs the IV pumps into my system. This isn't my first surgery—isn't even the first emergency surgery.

But it is the first time I'm not terrified.

If this is the end for me… I'll deal with it. Eventually. After the operation, I'm sure I'll need recovery time before starting physical therapy, and then time to regain normal function… I'll can worry about all of that later. *After* I wake up from surgery. After I see the doctor.

For now, I'm taking it a minute at a time. Amelia is curled up on a chair beside me, her hand in mine while she dozes. It's close to two o'clock in the morning, and there's no telling when they'll wheel me back for pre-op.

A nurse came by and helped me clean up a bit, so at least I'm not disgusted by my own stink anymore. I texted my mom the news, but she didn't respond—it's past her bedtime, so she'll probably see it when she wakes up.

Finally, close to four o'clock in the morning, an orderly and a nurse come to take me to pre-op. Amelia stirs, her eyes blinking open.

"Is it time?" she asks, her voice hoarse with sleep.

The nurse nods. "It'll be about two and a half hours. I'll show you to the waiting room."

My girlfriend stands, smoothing back my hair. "This is will go well. I'll see you after."

I love you. I almost say the words. But it's a reflex. Something to say when a scary thing happens.

It's too soon. I'm not in love with her, not yet. Am I?

Now isn't the time to figure it out.

"I'll be here when you get out," Amelia says. She presses a kiss to my forehead. "You'll do great."

I squeeze her hand, pulling her to me until she's close enough that I can kiss her for real.

"I—"

She nods. "It'll be okay."

But I shake my head. "No, I—" The words die in my throat. I can't verbalize it. Gulping, I try again. The words won't come.

"I know," she whispers. She kisses me again. "I'll be here when you get out."

The nurse clears her throat. "It's time to go."

Amelia steps back. I blow out a breath and transfer to the wheelchair.

The orderly is silent as she wheels me through the hospital. It's not my first rodeo, that's for sure. After a few times under the knife, the fear dulls somewhat, but the pain is as sharp as ever.

Time becomes a little hazy. Before long, they take me into the operating room and helping me onto the table. The last thing I remember before they give me the good drugs is Dr. Hudson leaning over me.

"It'll be okay, son," he says. "Just a quick nap, and you'll be better than ever."

And then they pump the meds into my system, and I'm out like a light.

———

I wake up disoriented. The hospital room is unfamiliar, yet looks like every other hospital room I've ever been in. A machine beeps steadily, and there's an IV taped to my hand. My leg is numb. That's good. It will probably hurt like a bitch when the meds wear off.

There's a soft snuffling beside me, and I glance over to find Amelia contorted on the small sofa. Her Kindle is beside her, teetering on the edge of the cushion, like it's about to fall off.

She looks beautiful, even with her dark hair pulled back into a lopsided ponytail, and her makeup smeared all over her face. She stayed all night. She stayed by my side for as long as they'd let her, and now she's here again.

And I know, it's not because she's my patient advocate. She's here because of what we share, and I don't take that for granted.

Slowly, she stirs, and her eyes blink open a few times. She focuses on me, and a wide smile splits her face.

"You're awake," she says. Unfolding herself from the couch, she comes to my side, smoothing my hair back again. She's never done it as much as she has in the last twelve hours, but I can't deny how much I like it.

"Mm. Come here." I reach for her until her hand lands in mine, and I tug her down to meet me for a closed-mouth kiss. The inside of my mouth is sleep-sour, and I won't subject her to it.

Amelia pulls back, her hand cupping my face. "How're you feeling?"

"Better, now." I scoot over in the uncomfortable hospital bed as much as I can. "Come sit."

She pauses.

"Please. I need you." My voice breaks.

Her soft sigh melts the tension in her shoulders. She

perches on the edge of the bed, and I tug at her legs until she swings them up onto the bed.

I wind my non-IV arm behind her, curling her into my body. She rests her head on my chest, her palm landing on my abs.

"Much better," I declare, burying my face in her hair. She smells sweet, like marshmallows and hot cocoa—it's her favorite body wash—and more importantly, she smells like *home.*

We both drift off, dozing in and out of consciousness. I'm dimly aware of a nurse coming by to check on me, but I fall back asleep to the sound of her clucking at us.

A knock on the door wakes me up, and I blink through fuzzy contact lenses at Dr. Hudson, wearing a white coat over his scrubs.

"How're you feeling, son?" he asks, glancing between me and Amelia with a question on his face.

She's out like a light, though, and I don't have the heart to wake her.

"Pain meds are great," I tell him honestly.

He hums. "We'll get you a script for the flight home."

"Can I go back today?"

"We need to monitor you for twenty-four hours. If everything goes well, you can fly home tomorrow or the day after."

It's only then that I notice the woman beside him, wearing a white coat over her dark green scrubs.

"Mr. McKittrick. I'm Dr. Iglesias, and I'm overseeing your recovery for the next day or so."

"Nice to meet you." I'd shake her hand, but my right arm is currently trapped under Amelia's sleeping form.

"We'll make sure you're stable enough to travel as soon as possible," Dr. Iglesias continues. "I know you're itching to get back to Boston. The major concern right now is blood clots. Flying could exacerbate it. As soon as you're past the risk window, we'll get you sent home."

"Thanks." I swallow. "And recovery timeline?"

"You'll need to wear a cast for four to twelve weeks," Dr. Hudson says. That puts me out for the remainder of the season, and the entirety of the postseason.

I wince.

"I know. You'll be non-weight bearing for a few weeks, and then we'll assess and re-cast if necessary. You'll have a lot of physical therapy." His mouth curves into a wry smile. "Not that it'll be a hardship for you, eh?"

"We don't—she doesn't do my PT," I clarify. "We keep our relationship strictly professional at work."

Dr. Hudson snorts. "Sure, son."

I flush, thinking about that day in her office. We definitely didn't keep things *strictly professional* that day.

"You won't tell anyone?"

"None of my business," he says, lifting his hands in the air. "You might want to get ahead of it, though, before anyone else finds out. You and I both know not much stays a secret in that dressing room for long."

"She's not ready."

Truth be told, I don't know if I am, either. So much would change, for both of us. It's not like we can un-tell the secret. And what if we break up?

I don't want to break up. But I didn't want to get divorced, either, and that happened anyway. And *everyone* keeps asking about it. It would be worse with Amelia—everyone knows her and likes her. What if my teammates pick sides? What if they choose her over me?

Maybe it's a good thing my contract finishes at the end of this season. I'll go to another team and start fresh.

Well. Maybe I can find another team that'll take a chance on a guy with four knee surgeries and an Achilles tear under his belt. Maybe I can find someone willing to gamble on a senior citizen hockey player.

My mood sours.

But I don't want to leave Boston. It's been my home for going on eight years. I like it there. I have a home.

And I have Amelia. I don't have to start worrying about the end. There's no reason to borrow trouble before we're ready.

If she wants to keep us a secret, I'll deal with it. I won't push her before she tells me she wants this.

When it's time to come clean, we'll do it—together.

twenty-eight

· · ·

Amelia

AFTER TWO DAYS in the hospital, Jason is cleared to fly home, and we board a charter flight back to Boston. I went back to the hotel to shower and sleep—at his insistence—and otherwise, spent every waking hour at his bedside. I think he's getting a little sick of me. Three days of togetherness with all the pain he's in isn't easy to deal with.

Dr. Iglesias says everything looks great. He'll be in a cast for a few weeks before he can try putting weight on it again, but for now, all he can do is rest.

Right now, we're sitting side-by-side on the jet. I wanted my own seat to give him space, but he insisted we share the bench seat. He pulled me close, wrapped his arm around me, and promptly fell asleep.

We won't have very many moments like this in the immediate future. I'm sure the guys will troop in and out of his apartment, ready to help and entertain him. What will he do when the guys are on road trips? There's nobody else on the Injured Reserve list right now, and hopefully, it stays that way. But he'll be alone even more.

Zac prefers not to travel with the team since his kids are so young, so he'll probably take the lead on Jason's PT. I'd volunteer to do it, but it's not a good idea for a laundry list of reasons. I'd much rather be his girlfriend than his punching bag, and coming back from this injury will tax him in ways he hasn't considered yet.

I've already texted Tyler, who delivered a full fridge of food to Jason's apartment. I also arranged for our cleaning crew to go in and do a deep clean. Even though he has a cleaning crew of his own, I don't think it occurred to him to schedule them, so I took the liberty of arranging it. I don't want to micromanage his life; I only want to make this recovery as smooth as possible for him.

Jason jerks awake, his entire body jolting. I pat his chest, trying to soothe him.

"What time is it?" he mumbles.

"We have about an hour and a half left." Time zones have no meaning in the air.

"Fuck. I had the weirdest dream." He scrubs a hand over his face. "I'm sorry. Did I wake you?"

"I was reading." It's hard for me to fall asleep on planes, which is not great when half my life is on the road.

"I just want to be home," he groans, adjusting his ankle, which is propped on the seat across from us. "I want to take a shower and crawl into my own bed."

Swallowing, I ask the question I've avoided. "Do you want me to stay with you?"

He squints at me. "You're not talking about sexy times, are you?"

I shake my head. "Do you want me to stay over and help take care of you?"

Jason scowls. "I'm not an invalid."

"No, but you're on crutches for the foreseeable future. I don't mind staying. But we'll need to have a story ready."

"I wish it was for some sexy times," he grumbles.

Right now, he's on so many pain meds, it's out of the question. I don't think he could get it up, if he tried.

I pat his chest. "As soon as you're off the meds, I'll take care of you."

"I don't need taking care of." He huffs petulantly. "I'm fine."

"I was talking about a blowjob. But if you don't want one…" I pull my hand away from his pec.

He takes my hand, flattening it against his abs. "I didn't say that."

Hiding my smile against his chest, I burrow further into his side. "Your leg might be fucked, but I can still ride you. Just means we have to be careful."

His hand cups my face, catching my chin between his thumb and his forefinger. He tilts my face up until he can kiss me, his mouth devouring mine.

"You can ride me right now. The flight attendant isn't watching."

Laughing, I shake my head. "Not until you're off the pain meds."

Grumbling under his breath, he tightens his arm around me and kisses the top of my head. A grown man pouting shouldn't be this cute.

Then again, there isn't much he could do that I wouldn't find adorable.

I only want him to feel better. It might take a while before he finds himself again, but I'll be by his side the entire time—whether he likes it or not.

———

Three days later, and he doesn't like it. Not one bit.

"I'm going stir crazy here," he snaps. "I need to get out. I need to *move*."

"We can walk down the hallway again," I suggest.

Jason makes a face.

"Look, it's twelve degrees outside, and icy as fuck. The

last thing you need is to slip and injure yourself worse," I point out. "I can drive you to the practice facility if you want to hang out with the guys."

He scowls. "I don't need a babysitter."

I blow out a breath. "I know you don't. I'm offering. I have to run some errands, anyway, so I don't mind driving you over."

He's off the pain meds, and his right leg is fine, so in theory he can drive, but his mobility is still impaired. Getting in and out of the car with crutches is difficult.

"Fine," he grumbles. Heaving himself off the couch, he crutches his way into the bedroom. From my spot on the sofa, I watch as he drops his athletic shorts, his soft cock hanging between his legs as he struggles into a pair of boxer briefs and then a pair of joggers.

We haven't had sex yet. For all his eagerness on the plane, I gave him a hand job yesterday that turned into him pushing my hand away, not able to cross the finish line. I'm struggling not to take it personally.

He's in pain, especially now that he's off the meds, but I can't help feeling rejected. The rational part of my brain knows he has a lot going on right now, but it doesn't stop those negative, self-conscious thoughts from creeping in.

Once he's changed into a team long-sleeved shirt and a zip-up hoodie, he slips his right foot into his shoe, looking at me expectantly.

Grabbing my coat and purse, I follow him out the door, the electronic lock securing automatically. We take the elevator down to the lobby, and I leave him there as I hurry to my building's parking garage, pulling the car around the front for him.

Morning skate is over, and the guys are settling in for tape review right about now. It's my day off, so even if I wanted to hang out with the team, I have some things to take care of. Things I've been avoiding.

I drop Jason off at the entrance to the facility and wait until he's safely inside before pulling out, driving across town to the bookstore Vanessa recommended.

It's a small brick building in an old neighborhood, cutesy and cozy. There's a coffee cart in front of the shop, manned by a woman with a teal streak in her hair. I order a latte and browse through the store, taking it all in.

"Can I help you?" A curvy woman wearing a purple smock approaches, her dark eyes friendly. She wears her chocolate brown hair in a wavy style, and has a gold hoop through her nose. My eyes flick down to her name tag. SADIE. Just the person I was looking for.

"Vanessa and Jared said I should come introduce myself," I say. "I'm Amelia, a physical therapist with—"

"Oh, you work for the Grizzlies!" Sadie says. "Van told me all about you."

I gulp. "Good things?"

"Based on your TBR, yeah, you'll fit right in here," she says, a bright smile on her face.

She's dating the team's sports analyst, Jared Aviyente. When he saw me with my Kindle for the third time in three days, he suggested I reach out to Sadie about her book club. Vanessa overheard and agreed. She's been a member for years, and even Robby has come to a few meetings.

"I'm not good at... this." I wave my hand in the air. "Making friends." I pause. "Making friends with *women*."

To my surprise, Sadie grins. "That makes sense, especially given the hyper-masculine work environment. And Van said you have two brothers?"

"Well, one and his husband. But when I say I have two brothers who are married to each other, people get weirded out," I grin.

"Oh, we're going to get along so well," she says. "Come on to the back of the shop, and I'll show you where we set up for book club."

She launches into a spiel about the group of people who get together twice monthly for book club. Most of them are neurodivergent, but everyone is included regardless of disability. Rachel and Audrey, married to the two goaltenders, are both part of the book club, as is Hailey, MacGregor's sister. Gonzo's sister-in-law, Viv, is a member, too.

"We used to meet only once a month, but we found too many people had scheduling conflicts, so we opened it up to twice a month. BYOB—bring your own booze, not boyfriend." Sadie snickers. "We had an issue with that once."

"I don't know how often I'll make it. Between home games and road trips…"

"You'll come when you can," she says, patting my arm. "Van doesn't make it to every meetup, either. We know the score. Work comes first. It has to."

"So, we all read one book every two weeks?" I can do that, easy peasy.

Sadie shakes her head. "We don't have assigned reading. It's more of a social club where we talk about romance books and what we like and dislike. We hang out, we drink a little, snack a little, and at the end of the night, you hopefully leave with your well recharged."

I blink at her. "My well?"

"Social battery, people meter, whatever metaphor you use. You can't draw from an empty well; you have to refill it from time to time with the things that make you feel relaxed and at peace with yourself. That's our goal, to make you take a moment to pause and appreciate all the things you enjoy about your life."

"I like that," I admit. "I've been… well, it's been a rough few days."

She clucks sympathetically. "It'll get better."

Shrugging, I admit, "Yeah, but it'll take longer than I'd like."

"Anything I can do to help? Or anyone else?"

I shake my head. "Some things just take time."

Sadie pats my arm again. "Well, there's nothing a good book can't cure. Now tell me, how do you feel about grumpy-sunshine?"

My thoughts drift to my scowling hockey player. He's extra scowly these days, and there's nothing I can do to fix it; this is natural after an injury.

"Sign me the fuck up. I want all the books."

I let her lead me through the store, and before long, I've picked up four new paperbacks, plus a list of others to add to my Kindle. She also extracted a promise that I'd join the book club at their meetup next Thursday, since it happens to be my night off.

It's time to put down roots. I'm staying in Boston; it's time to start acting like it.

twenty-nine

· · ·

Jason

I'M ON THE SIDELINES. I can't work out; I can't go out on the ice; I can't travel on road trips. The list of things I can't do is longer than the list of what I can.

The other day, I yelled at Amelia. She was talking about finding a hobby, something to entertain me while I'm on leave, and all I did was snap at her about my life being over.

I'm not trying to ruin your life, she said. *I'm trying to save it.*

Hockey is my life, I'd shouted back.

Well, you're at the end of your career, so you better start thinking about what comes next.

It's been four days, and I haven't stopped thinking about it. What comes next? What do I do? All I know is hockey. Ever since I was in kindergarten, my life revolved around hockey. Other kids play a few sports before they commit, but not me; hockey was it for me from the very beginning. My dad had me in skates as soon as I could walk. It's my first love, my one true love. I love it more than I loved my ex-wife.

If I'm not a hockey player anymore, who am I?

When I was injured before, I never once considered what would happen if I didn't have hockey in my life. I was young. I had my entire life ahead of me.

I was an idiot.

The end is coming along a lot faster than I'd like. What will I do next? I can't sit on my ass for the rest of my life.

Later that night, I crawled to her and apologized. She accepted it, but she's been a little frosty with me since. I can't deny I deserve it. Shouting at a partner is disrespectful, and I never want her to think I don't respect and value her. She makes my life better; I don't know what I'd do without her in it.

Crutching through the training facility, I nod at Graham and Zac, eating lunch in the lounge. There's no sign of Amelia as I make my way to the medical bay.

Halfway there, Derek stops me. He jerks his head towards his office, and I limp my way over.

"How you doing?" he asks, closing the door behind him.

"I'm fine."

The athletic trainer rolls his eyes. "Yeah. Sure. Let's pretend I believe that. When do you see Dr. Hudson?"

"In five minutes."

He winces in sympathy. "You'll be fine."

"Sure. Let's pretend I believe that," I snark back.

Derek erupts into a belly laugh. "So, you do have a personality, then."

"What's that supposed to mean?"

"You've been kind of down lately. Not engaging with the guys, keeping to yourself…"

"There's a lot on my mind," I deflect.

"Did something happen with Amelia?"

My head jerks up as my heart rate skyrockets. "What do you mean?"

"She's been different ever since you came back. I thought she could handle being a patient advocate, but maybe…"

"Nothing happened," I snap. "She was the perfect professional the entire time."

Except for when she crawled into my hospital bed. But I asked her to do it.

And I'd ask her again, every time.

Derek eyes me, pursing his lips.

"She was great. Perfectly supportive without being smothering."

"I noticed you don't go to her for PT. Only Zac and Graham."

I wince. "So?"

"So, if there were any issues…"

"There aren't any," I tell him firmly.

"But if there were, you could tell me," he says.

I scrub a hand over my face, preparing to bend the truth. "I have a thing for her. It's inappropriate, so nothing will come of it. But it means I can't work with her."

His eyebrows go up. "Seriously?"

"It's better for all of us if I keep my distance."

"I thought you couldn't stand her."

"Kind of the opposite."

He chokes out a laugh. "As long as there's no funny business…"

I shake my head. "I'd never make her feel uncomfortable or unsafe. I just can't go to her for PT."

Not without destroying our relationship. She means too much to me for that.

"Understood," Derek nods.

He dismisses me, and I hobble along to Dr. Hudson's office. I hop up onto the exam table, and wait for his update.

Oh, fuck. I told Derek last week I was seeing someone. And now he knows I have feelings for Amelia. What if he puts the pieces together? Doc did. Gonzo did. Who the hell else will figure it out before she's ready to announce it?

My heart starts to race, and I feel vaguely nauseous. There's a faint ringing in my ears. Did I just ruin this? Will she forgive me?

The door opens, but I'm too deep into my panic to recognize it. My throat constricts and I swallow, trying to clear the lump.

"McKittrick?" Doc's voice sounds far away. "Jason!"

My head jerks up, but it's hard to concentrate on him. Everything is blurry. I blink a few times, but it's not my contact lenses.

Doc snaps his fingers in front of my face, drawing my attention. "Breathe, son," he says firmly.

I draw in a ragged breath, exhaling through my nose.

"And again," he instructs.

As I do, everything starts to come back into focus.

"Do you want to talk about what just happened?" he asks.

I shake my head. "What was that?"

"Well, it looked like a panic attack. Have you had one before?" There's no judgment on his face.

"No. Never."

"Hmm." Doc sits back on his chair, studying me. "What were you thinking about when I came in? Your ankle?"

Swallowing the lump in my throat, I quietly admit, "Amelia. I think I fucked up."

"Well, most likely, yes," he says, with a chuckle. "You're not infallible."

"No, I mean… I said something I shouldn't have."

"So, you'll apologize."

"Like it's that easy."

"If she loves you, it is," Doc says. He picks up his tablet. "Now, let's talk about your ankle."

After taking off the cast, he does a visual examination before examining the incision site. The stitches have dissolved, the fresh scar a vivid reminder of what happened. With time, it'll fade. The pain will go away. But I won't be able to escape the memories.

"Am I clear to start walking on it?" I ask.

"You know the timeline is weeks, not days," he says. "You're out for the rest of the season, Jason."

Groaning, I cover my hands with my face. "No."

"I'm sorry, son. I know it's not what you want." He pats my knee. "Even if the team goes deep into the post-season, you won't be back."

"But I *can* come back?"

"If it's what you want, yes. We can help you rehab and get back into shape." Doc pauses. "But if you decide you're done… that's okay, too."

"I don't want to go out this way. Not like this."

"We can't always choose how we go out. It's not always on our terms."

I swallow. This is the end of my hockey career. I know deep in my soul I won't get another contract. Even if I pour my entire being into rehabbing, I'm too old, too injured, too slow.

This chapter of my life is over. But the next is just beginning. Amelia. A life post-hockey.

Clearing my throat, I meet Doc's eye. "In that case, I need a referral to a urologist."

"Oh? Are you having issues?"

"I want a vasectomy."

Amelia doesn't want kids. Neither do I. Why should I needlessly put her at risk when we're both sure about what we want for our lives?

Dr. Hudson frowns. "Are you sure? You have your whole life ahead of you."

To him, this is sudden, but I've been chewing on it for weeks. I don't have a problem using condoms, and Amelia has an IUD. Eventually, though, she'll take the fertility drugs again in preparation for another surrogacy. I'll hold her hand the entire time. But I won't put her at risk.

"Yeah, but I don't want kids."

My revelation a few months ago in Amelia's exam room

opened my eyes. I can have a fulfilling life without kids. I can have a fulfilling life without *hockey*.

"I've thought about it for a while, but I didn't want to do anything during the season that would keep me from playing." Swallowing against the lump in my throat at the idea I won't play again, I focus on the positive. "If I don't have to worry about missing any more games, I can do the procedure now. Get it over with."

Doc surveys me seriously. "You're sure this is what you want?"

"Positive."

"And she's not pressuring you into this?"

I shake my head. "This is for me."

"All right, then. I'll write you the referral."

thirty

• • •

Amelia

THE LOUNGE IS devoid of players as my friends and I gather for lunch. We ordered in for a change, and as Joaquin, Patrice, Robby, Vanessa, and I catch up on our respective days, a sense of contentment washes over me.

Jason and I had our first big fight the other day. He apologized, but I can't get it out of my mind. What if this is too much for him? What if I can't navigate being his girlfriend instead of his physical therapist? I don't want him to be my patient, but I can't turn off that side of my brain.

"What's wrong, babe?" Robby asks as he scoops some lo mein onto my plate.

"Nothing's wrong." I serve him some of the broccoli beef in front of me.

"You heaved the biggest sigh in the history of the world," he says.

"I'm fine," I mutter.

"You don't seem fine," Joaquin says.

Glaring at him isn't as satisfying as I thought.

He innocently lifts his hands. "I'm just saying. You seem a little down."

"For the last few days," Patrice adds.

Swallowing my courage, I admit, "Had a fight with someone."

"Ah, man troubles," Robby says sagely. "Been there, done that."

"Yeah, I don't need to hear about your exploits with my brother."

He laughs. "For once, I was talking about someone else. Come on, tell us all about him."

I toy with the food on my plate. "It was only a fight."

"Yeah, but you've been seeing him for months," Patrice says. "Surely, you've fought before."

Blinking at her, my face heats. "How did you know?"

"Because you walk around this place with your heart in your eyes," Vanessa points out. "You're always smiling at your phone. Whoever you're seeing is good for you."

"So," Joaquin presses. "Who is he?"

I shove a giant bite of broccoli into my mouth, making an exaggerated show of chewing.

"Do we know him?" Robby tacks on.

I shake my head.

"How'd you meet? You're always working," Vanessa points out. "You take the most road trips of all three PTs."

"I like to travel," I mumble.

"Bullshit," Patrice says. "Nobody likes this schedule."

She, Joaquin, and Robby travel for every single road trip, whereas Vanessa and I both have a team who rotates on-call schedules.

Although, now that she's eight months pregnant, she isn't traveling anymore. Scott and Jacky have taken over the rotation.

The team plays at home tonight, but then we're off on another away series. It's the first time I'm on the road while Jason will stay at home. I already miss him, which is kind of ridiculous. It's only a three-day trip.

But my friends won't let it rest.

"When do we get to meet this guy?" Robby asks.

"Never."

"How do we know he's good enough for you?" Joaquin adds.

"You trust that I can make my own decisions and won't tolerate someone disrespecting me," I tell him, with a simple shrug. "I don't see you asking any of the guys on the team if the women they're seeing are good enough for them."

Robby narrows his eyes. "We don't have that type of relationship with the players."

"Besides, it's none of our business because they aren't our friends. Not the way you are," Joaquin says. "This guy is part of your life and he has been for a few months. He's not a fling. He means something to you, so yeah, we want to meet him."

I roll my eyes. "I already have two overprotective brothers. I don't need any more."

"Oh, honey," Patrice says. "You think you have two? You have twenty-three guys on the team who would beat up anyone who looked at you funny. And that's not including all of the staff."

"No one will be beat up," I say firmly.

"So, how'd you meet him, anyway?" Vanessa asks.

Shaking my head, I avoid the question. "Pass the soy sauce, please."

"Amelia," Robby says quietly. "Do we know him?"

My face heats, and I open my mouth to deny it.

But the lounge door swings open, and the place is flooded with smelly, sweaty hockey players, fresh from a yoga class.

"I'm done talking about this," I tell them.

Gonzo and Sinclair approach with Larsson. The Swede ducks down to kiss his wife on the cheek, his palm rubbing her swollen belly. They snuck away to the courthouse a few weeks ago and made things official. He hasn't stopped smiling since.

"Hey, Meels. Patty," Gonzo says, ruffling my hair. Patrice glares at him, and he innocently lifts his hands. "Don't worry, I won't touch your hair."

"Or mine," I mutter, ruffling it back into place. It takes work to make the waves last longer than thirty minutes.

"Sorry, sorry," Gonzo says. "It's how we show love in our family."

Robby raises his eyebrows, and Joaquin snorts.

"Well, I'm honored you consider me your family," I start. Gonzo smirks. "But don't touch my hair."

"Let's all keep our hands to ourselves," Jason's voice booms out.

The room falls silent as he crutches into the lounge.

"Do we need a reminder about the workplace sexual harassment policy?" he adds, glaring at Gonzo.

"Nope. We're good," the burly hockey player says, taking a step back from me. "Right, Amelia?"

"We're great," I say, with a forced smile.

Jason grunts, glaring at his assembled teammates. "That goes for all of you. I won't tolerate harassment of any of our staff members. They are here to do a job, same as all of us. Don't make their lives harder."

"Yes, Captain," a few players mumble.

MacGregor clears his throat. "How's your leg?"

Jason sighs. "I'm out for the rest of the year."

"Shit, man," Logan says, shaking his head. "I'm sorry."

"We'll just have to win the Cup for you, then," Easton says.

Jason forces a brittle, bitter smile. "Yes, you will."

An awkward chuckle echoes throughout the room.

"I'm not going anywhere. I'll still be here day in and day out with you," he says firmly. "Nothing has to change." His eyes fall to me, and then slip past to Robby, who's staring at him with an inscrutable expression on his face. "Okay, back to lunch."

thirty-one

. . .

Jason

IT'S lonely being on my own. This isn't the first time I've been on the Injured Reserve list, but it is the first time no other players are injured at the same time.

Doc scheduled me in with a urologist. I have a consult with him next week, but I haven't had a chance to talk to Amelia about my decision. When she gets back from the road trip, I'll do it. I'm totally not avoiding the conversation, not at all.

There's a knock on my door, and I crutch over to let Tyler in. He's carrying a tote bag in each hand, Ainsley strapped to his chest in a pink carrier.

"Thanks for coming by," I tell him.

He goes straight to the kitchen, unloading the bags. "Thanks for being flexible with timing."

Tomorrow is opening day for baseball season, and the Bulldogs are playing at home. I don't blame him for wanting to be with his husband rather than slaving over a hot stove all day.

Even if he does have staff to help put together the meals, he's still involved. And he deserves a day off. Amelia mentioned he does meal prep for sixteen hockey players and twelve guys on the baseball team, plus other clients.

Tyler puts all the meals in the fridge, which is empty aside from a few apples, a six-pack of beer, and a bottle of Amelia's favorite wine. I'm not much of a moscato drinker, but she likes the occasional glass while she soaks in my tub, so I buy it for her.

He blinks at the label on the bottle, but doesn't otherwise comment.

"How's the ankle?" he asks.

Ainsley squawks in her carrier, kicking her chubby little legs, and he runs a hand over her belly.

"She's so big." I avoid the question.

"Eight months," Tyler agrees. "Meeting all her milestones like a pro."

"Have you thought about more?"

"More kids?"

I nod.

"Yeah, but it's up to Amelia and her timeline. We're not rushing her," he says. "And if she decides she doesn't want to do it again, we'll find another surrogate. We already have embryos stored."

"It's incredible that she donated her eggs. That she carried Ainsley."

"Biology sucks sometimes, but it can also be really great," he says. "I couldn't give Brandon a baby, so she donated our family gene pool. She donated her body to us. I can never repay her for the gift she gave me."

"Amelia and I are seeing each other," I blurt out. "We're together."

Tyler laughs. "Yeah, I know."

I blink. "You do?"

"You started closing your blinds around the same time she started seeing you. She's always happy when she looks out the window at your place. Talks about you as *Jason* and not

McKittrick, like the rest of the players." He shakes his head. "It didn't take long to put it together."

"I'm sorry we didn't tell you."

"You don't have to take responsibility for her decisions. Because I'm fairly certain it was her decision, not yours." Tyler laughs again. "She didn't want to lie to us, and she didn't want to ask us to keep her secret. We would have, though. No questions asked. We both know what it's like to hide a part of yourself, and not being sure how other people will take the news."

"I'm crazy about her," I admit.

"And would it bother you? Her being pregnant with our baby?"

"Not in the slightest. I think it's amazing."

"It means you and her having kids…"

"Not in the cards for us," I say firmly.

He raises an eyebrow.

"Neither of us wants kids. Our lives aren't conducive to a stable family life, anyway."

"Have you thought about what you're going to do?" He nods at my ankle. "After?"

"Still thinking it over." I put a call in to my agent, but he hasn't gotten back to me aside from a vague, "we'll talk soon."

"Well, there's one thing I learned from spending so much time with athletes over the years," he says.

"What's that?"

"The entire world is open to you. You've made millions of dollars, the kind of money most people only dream about. You can do anything you want with your life. You can go back to school. You can start a new career. The only limit is your imagination."

"I never thought I'd have a life after hockey. I never even considered it. Probably should have."

"Well, that was then, and this is now. You can only move forward." He pauses. "Do you intend to stay in Boston?"

"It's my home."

"Aren't you from Chicago?"

I shrug. "I haven't lived there since I was sixteen, when I went away for the juniors. It's not my home. Not anymore. This is. This is where I want to be."

His eyes narrow, studying me. "And I'm sure it doesn't hurt that Amelia is here too?"

It's a test; one I'm sure I need to pass.

"Wherever she wants to go, I'll follow."

"Wow. You're serious about her."

It's the honest truth. I'm not sweet-talking her brother into liking me—hopefully, he already does. I'm laying my cards on the table.

"I don't know that I'm ready to get married anytime soon, not after the disaster that was my divorce. But when I look at my future, she's in it. I'm by her side."

Tyler hums.

"What?"

"You're by her side," he says. "Not that she's by your side."

"She's the catch in the situation. Like you said, the whole world is open to me. Wherever she wants to be, that's where I'll go."

But I think she'll want to stay here. After all, her brothers are here. Her niece. She built a life here. She's close to her coworkers. She's finally putting down roots.

Ainsley squirms in her carrier, her chubby face contorted.

"Oh, shit," Tyler says. "I have six point seven seconds before she starts shrieking. Gotta go."

"Come by anytime," I tell him. "All three of you are welcome anytime."

He nods seriously, clapping me on the back. "You're a good man, McKittrick. I'm glad Amelia picked you."

His praise blooms something deep within my chest. I open my mouth, but I'm cut off by an insistent wail.

"Overstayed our welcome," he says, bouncing his knees to soothe the baby. "I'll look at the calendar, and you'll come over for family dinner."

It's not a request.

"I'll be there," I promise. "For as long as she'll have me."

thirty-two

. . .

Amelia

ROBBY HAS BEEN GIVING me weird looks all week. Every time I turn around, he's watching me, a furrow in his brow. On our road trip, he made a point to sit beside me on our flights, and in the few days we've been home, he's asked me to lunch each day. I always have a carefully crafted excuse for why I can't be alone with him.

In the pit of my stomach, I know he knows. And if he asks me outright, I won't lie to him. He doesn't deserve to be deceived. I just have to hope that he'll agree to keep my secret.

Derek calls me, Zac, and Graham in for our morning staff meeting, checking on our caseloads. I don't think anything of it until, as he's closing the meeting, he adds one last remark.

"Don't forget to do your sexual harassment training by the end of the week." His eyes linger on me, and I keep my face carefully neutral. "It's assigned in the learning module for all staff members."

"You got it, boss," Graham says, giving him a salute.

"Didn't we just do it?" Zac asks.

"Management decided it's time for a refresher," Derek

says. "The training should take less than half an hour. Knock it out, and we can go on with our day."

I nod, my stomach swirling with nerves.

Someone knows.

Someone high in management knows. What the hell do we do now?

The only good thing about Jason's injury is that we can't work together until his cast is removed and he's cleared for light movement. There's no chance of *fraternizing* when he's banned from travel and isn't playing.

It's still shitty, though. I don't want to spend time outside of work with any of the players, only my boyfriend.

Now that the team is home, there's a steady stream of visitors at Jason's place. I haven't be spent the night since I got back. The guys are constantly at their captain's door, inviting themselves over for dinner or video games or a chat.

As happy as I am that he has a support network, I selfishly want him all to myself. I don't want to share him.

But this is part and parcel of being captain. He has to be there to lend an ear and support his teammates. I just wish I could be with him and not relegated to my apartment—or worse, sitting quietly in his bedroom, like his dirty little secret.

I could go to management. I could tell them we're together.

Except I don't know if *he* is ready for that. There has been no mention of going down to HR. He didn't even tell me he talked to Tyler about us; my brother told me, and as glad as I am to know they approve of us, I wish it was something we did together. No, Jason's kept everything close to his chest; almost too close.

He won't talk about what happens next. About what he'll do after the season's over. Will he try for another contract?

Jason is on my mind all through my morning patients, and as I walk into the lounge to fill my water bottle, I find him sitting with MacGregor and Easton, the two assistant captains.

Nodding at the guys, I make my way to the water filter, filling the bottle. I can hear the low murmur of voices, the words indistinct.

I head back to my office to input my notes on Sinclair's wrist when there's a knock on the open door. Swiveling on the stool, my stomach swoops when Jason crutches his way into the small office, closing the door behind him.

My mouth runs dry. "What are you doing here?"

"I need to talk to you," he says. "And since I can't seem to get five minutes alone with you at home…"

"You've been busy." There's no judgment in my voice, only resignation.

"Yeah." Jason clears his throat. "I made a decision, and it's something that impacts you, so I need you to not freak out about it."

"Okay…" My heart rate ricochets up.

"You're certain you don't want kids, right? One hundred percent?" There's a furrow between his brow. "Because if this is a work thing…"

"I don't want kids," I tell him. "Yes, I value my career more than having a child. But I also don't *want* a child of my own. I have a niece I adore. That's enough for me."

He lets out a gusty breath. "Okay. Then, I need a favor."

"Oh?"

"You're off on Thursday. It's the league mandated day off."

Carefully, I nod. Where's he going with this?

"Do you mind…" He swallows. "What I'm trying to say is, I need a ride."

"A ride? To the doctor?"

"Yeah. I'm seeing a specialist."

I blink. "Okay, I'm missing something here. Because

you're acting like this is the end of the world. It's not. Your ankle will heal. You'll be fine."

Jason shakes his head. "It's not for my ankle. I have an appointment with a urologist."

"Okay?"

"For a vasectomy," he blurts.

My eyebrows go sky high. "What?"

"I don't want kids. And you don't want kids. And I'm out for the season," he rushes out. "So, why not get it done? Get it over with?"

"You want to have a vasectomy because *I* don't want kids?"

"I don't want them, either," he says. "If you did… If you did, it's something I'd consider, but it would probably be the end for us. At the very least, I'd resent you for forcing me into it."

I flinch.

"But I don't want them. Neither do you. I'm fine with Ainsley and my nieces and nephews," he hurries to add. "Kids can still be part of our lives without being *our* children."

"So, you're having a vasectomy," I say slowly.

He nods. "I know in the grand scheme of things, it's a minor procedure. A bit of local anesthetic, and I'll be fine. But I'd like you to be there."

"To hold your hand?" I tease, trying to get my bearings.

"Yeah, Amelia," Jason says, with a shy smile. "I'd like you to hold my hand."

Swallowing my fears, I rise from my stool and approach him. We don't touch at work; not after what happened in this very room all those months ago.

But I can't stop myself from fisting his shirt and tugging until he ducks down enough that I can kiss him.

It's been days since we've been alone together. Two weeks since we last had sex on the day of his injury. I *miss* him. He's right in front of me. He's so close, but there's so much separating us.

Jason groans into the kiss, his tongue slipping past my lips to tangle with mine. I wrench back, meeting his eyes.

"You're sure about this?" I ask.

"I've never been more sure about anything in my life," he says.

I go to kiss him again, but before I can, there's a knock on the door.

Taking a step back, I smooth his shirt from where I gripped the soft cotton, fix my hair, and open the door.

"Ready for me?" Jenkins asks, a cocky smirk on his face. He's shirtless, wearing a pair of athletic shorts and slides with socks. His eyes widen at the sight of his captain in my office. "Hey, McKittrick. How's the ankle?"

"I'm fine," he says firmly. He opens his mouth like he wants to say something, and then closes it again.

Jenkins pushes past him into the office, laying on the bed. "How do you want me?"

Jason's face contorts in fury.

"Right there is fine," I say calmly. "Your elbow shouldn't take me long to deal with."

"Does that mean your day is almost done?" Jenkins asks, propping his head up on his left arm, the angle making his biceps bulge. His muscles do nothing for me. "Maybe we can hang out after, grab some dinner."

"I have plans," I tell him, pulling up his file on my tablet.

Jason lingers just inside the doorway, and I raise my eyebrows at him.

"Maybe another time," Jenkins says, not dissuaded in the slightest.

"I don't think my boyfriend would like that very much," I say lightly.

Jenkins' smirk grows wider. "Bring him along."

Chancing a glance at Jason, he's clenching his fists, about

ten seconds away from barging into my office and punching his teammate in the face.

That's one way to tell people about us.

"Look, I'm not into sharing or parties." My kink of showing off for Jason through our windows is one thing. I'm not interested in full-on exhibitionism in either a public or private setting.

The hockey player on my table laughs. "Amelia. I'm asking you to hang out. You're cool, but if you're seeing someone, I respect that. Doesn't mean we can't be friends."

"I'll think about it," I finally say.

"You should. We're on the road so much, it helps if we like each other and get along." He shrugs, as best he can while laying on my table. "We're all a family here. Isn't that what McKittrick always says? We can all hang out and have fun. It doesn't have to be more than it is."

Humming, I start to work on his elbow. My eyes dart toward the doorway, but Jason is gone, the door ajar.

What is he thinking?

thirty-three

· · ·

Jason

I **WANT** to punch Parker Jenkins in his stupid fucking face. And since that's not a thought I should have toward my teammate, I decide to punish myself by setting up shop in the stands overlooking the rink.

There's still a half hour before practice starts. The barn is quiet, empty. I like it like this.

Jenkins is young, in his second full season with the team. He's still learning. He might not have intended to proposition Amelia, or maybe he did and had the sense to walk it back, but who will teach him if I'm not here? There's still so much to learn, both on and off the ice.

The fury that laced through me when he asked her out... She shouldn't be subjected to that, not at work.

But she shut him down. Without a second thought, she shut him down.

Maybe she doesn't have one foot out the door, after all. Maybe she really is as invested in this as me.

What am I going to do with her? How long will she want to keep us a secret?

Derek knows I'm seeing someone. Jenkins knows she's

seeing someone. How long until someone puts two and two together?

I want to be with her. I want a future with her. When I told Tyler I wasn't ready to consider marriage, I meant it. But that doesn't mean I'm afraid of commitment. If anything, I'm afraid of *over* committing. What if I want this more than she does? What if this is simply a fun way for her to pass the time, and now that I'm not on the road with her every week, she forgets about me?

I did the long-distance thing. I did the heavy travel thing. The road gets lonely, but being left behind hurts more.

Will she still love me when I'm home all the time? When I don't have hockey occupying my every thought?

Wait a second. *Love*? Who said anything about love?

But immediately, I shake my head. I can't kid myself.

I'm in love with Amelia Owen. Even though half the time she drives me crazy, I'm still one hundred percent irrevocably in love with her.

Now, I only have to figure out how to tell her.

Footsteps announce the arrival of another person, and I nod at Coach Turner as he approaches.

"How you doing?" he asks, taking a seat beside me on the uncomfortable metal bleacher.

"Hanging in there." I still feel hollow at the end of my hockey career. I don't know what to do next. There are *too many* options rather than not enough.

The world is my oyster, but all I want is to be a happy little clam with Amelia.

Hockey, health, and Amelia, that's all I want. And not necessarily in that order.

"Doc says you're out for the season," Coach says. "And I know with the contract situation..."

"I think I'm done," I admit quietly. "I haven't told my agent yet, but we all know I can't get the type of deal I want."

"And what is it you want?"

Coach isn't involved in contract negotiations; that's between the GM and my agent. But he can give input.

"I don't want to give up hockey. I'm not ready to lose that chapter," I tell him. "But I want to stay in Boston. My life is here. I don't want to start over with a new team, jockeying for playing time in a new system. I don't know that my knee will hold up much longer, not to mention this mess with my Achilles."

He hums. "When you zoom out and look at your life, what do you want?"

Amelia.

And hockey.

I want them both.

When I fall silent, Coach tries something else. "You want to stay with the Grizzlies?"

"This team is my family. It's my home." My eight years with the Grizzlies were the best and worst years of my personal life. I played the best hockey of my career. I have friends who are more like family. No other dressing room I've ever been in is like the one we have here.

"You know, we have some open positions within the team," he says.

I freeze. "What do you mean?"

"Kelly is moving on. His wife's pregnant, and she wants to move closer to her family in Columbus. He put in his notice, and he's leaving at the end of the season." Josh Kelly is on the coaching staff. He played with the Grizzlies fifteen years ago, then went to Ottawa for a bit, and returned to our team as a coach.

Swallowing the lump in my throat, I curl my hands into fists to hide their shaking. "What are you saying?"

"I think you'd make a damn fine Player Development Coordinator," Coach says.

"What would that entail?" I hold my breath.

"A lot of what you've been doing as captain, simply in a different capacity. Working with the younger players, especially on developing their skills. Helping the veteran players stay consistent. Being a sounding board."

"And I'd still travel with the team?"

"Yep. We'd need you on the road. There will be some rotation, but you'd be with us more games than you wouldn't." Coach eyes me. "Is that an issue?"

I'd be on the road again. I'd be on the road *with Amelia.*

"Not at all."

"Whatever happens, whether you go out on the Long Term Injured Reserve list or you try to make a comeback, you're mine until your contract expires on June thirtieth. I expect you to commit to physical therapy and rehab, and do everything the trainers tell you."

"Yes, Coach."

"The salary is peanuts compared to what you're earning now, but it's very much a livable wage. You'll be comfortable, even without what you've hopefully saved." He clears his throat. "Take some time to think it over. We haven't advertised the position yet, but if you want it, it's yours."

"Thank you. I'll definitely think it over."

"You'll be all right, McKittrick," Coach says. "You'll land on your feet."

I wince, picking up my crutches. "We'll see."

"You will," he says confidently.

I'll think it over, but I'm already fairly certain I'll take the job. If nothing else, it keeps me close to hockey—and Amelia.

With that in mind, I find myself walking through the training facility to the office suite. Vanessa is in her cubicle, rubbing a hand over her swollen belly, with discomfort on her face. She's due any day now.

"McKittrick," she says, looking up and smiling at me. "What's up?"

"I need some advice."

She frowns. "How can I help?"

Shaking my head, my eyes flick to the ring on her finger before I meet her gaze. "It's something only you can help with."

thirty-four

. . .

Amelia

JASON WANTS A VASECTOMY. I don't know how to feel about it.

On the one hand, I don't want kids, but can't take any permanent birth control measures if I want to carry another kid for Tyler and Brandon. Jason having this procedure helps minimize risk for both of us, especially with the intense hormones they'll put me on pre-implantation.

At the same time, we've only been together for a few months. It's a lot of pressure to put on a new relationship. Why should my decision not to have kids mean he takes a permanent measure?

But *he* doesn't want kids. If he did, he wouldn't do it. He's putting his own needs first—and it just happens to benefit me. *Us.*

"Are we going to talk about it?" Tyler asks.

We're at a baseball game, cheering on Brandon and his teammates from the family suite. Ainsley is asleep, tuckered out from the excitement of the first inning. Now, it's the bottom of the fourth, and although the score is 1-1, the Bulldogs are playing some excellent baseball.

"Talk about what?" I ask.

"Why you haven't gone to Jason's lately."

I sigh. "He's busy."

"Too busy for you?" His eyebrows arch up.

"The team comes first, and I'm tired of hiding in his bedroom for hours when they come over to cheer him up." I'm trying not to be bitter about it. It's part of the deal. "I'm just tired of hiding it. The sneaking around thing gets old."

"So, are things fizzling out? Or is he not prioritizing you?"

I shake my head. "It's me. I took a step back."

Tyler shifts in his seat. "So, if you were at his place, and the guys came over… what would happen?"

"Well, I'd *like* to hang out with them. All of them." I play with my Bulldogs ball cap. "I don't want to be his dirty little secret."

"So don't. Go public."

"My job…"

"There are protocols in place. Go down to HR and sign the form," Tyler says.

"It's not that easy."

"Isn't it?" He glances at me from the corner of his eyes, and then flicks his attention back to the field, where Minnesota is up to bat. "Why are you so skittish? Do you think he's not as invested as you are?"

Reaching for my beer, I gulp down about half the extra-large cup. "He wants a vasectomy," I blurt out.

Tyler arches an eyebrow. "And that's a bad thing?"

"He asked me if I wanted kids first."

"But you don't." He runs his hand over Ainsley's back, snuggled against his chest in her carrier. "You've never wanted kids."

"Yeah, but he asked *me* before making that decision, even though he doesn't want them."

"So, healthy communication is a bad thing?"

"It is when we've barely been dating."

My brother laughs. "Meels, you've been together since

November. Five and a half months isn't barely. It's plenty of time to get to know each other."

I purse my lips. "Yeah, but—"

"You have a *yeah, but* for everything," he says. "Every suggestion I make, you shut down. So, dig deep and ask yourself, why are you so against it? Why won't you let yourself be happy?"

I open my mouth, and then close it.

"I'm scared he'll leave," I finally say. "What if he regrets this decision? What if three years down the line, he decides he does want to have kids, and then he blames me?"

"Then, you guys can use a sperm donor, or go the adoption or foster route," Tyler says. "Just consider, though… if he wasn't sure about this, he wouldn't make the decision. What would you say if someone asked you the same things? If they expected you to change your mind?"

With a sigh, I admit, "I'd tear them a new one."

"So, maybe trust that he's thought it all through, and he's as sure about it as you are." He reaches over and squeezes my arm. "It'll all work out. Even if you decide he's not the guy for you, this decision is not on you. It's entirely on him."

"He has a lot of big decisions coming up."

"And he'll make them. He'll probably talk to you about them," he says. "Once you stop hiding, that is."

"I'm not hiding."

He cuts his eyes to me. "You sure about that?"

"Okay, so maybe I'm hiding a little bit," I cave, twisting the bill of my cap. "I'm scared."

"It's okay, if you're scared," Tyler says. "Do it anyway. Live your life. Love your life."

I freeze. "L-love?"

He pauses. "Oh. Are you not there yet?"

"I—I don't know."

"That's scary, too," my big brother says softly. "But when

you let yourself free-fall, when you accept it and live your truth… it's the best feeling in the world."

There's a lump in my throat, and I swallow a few times, trying to clear it. Do I love Jason? How would I know?

I certainly like him. I'm attracted to him. When he's around, my heart starts beating faster, and it's like I have tunnel vision, and he's the only one I can see. He's the first person I want to share all my news and gossip with, and he's the last thought on my mind before falling asleep. He makes my day better just for being in it, even when we're separated.

And the way he kisses me? It's like my entire body's on fire, all the time.

"Oh, *fuck*," I whisper.

"And there it is," Tyler says, with a smirk. "Figured some things out, huh?"

"Fuck off," I mutter, socking him in the arm. "Don't act like you've got everything figured out. You were a mess when you fell for Brandon."

"Yeah, and look which one of us is happily married now," he teases.

Rolling my eyes, I take another sip of my beer. "Yeah, yeah, your life is pretty damn perfect. You belong in a Disney movie."

"I'm not saying it's perfect. Brando and I still fight. We have bad days." He shrugs, rubbing his hand over his daughter's back. "But there are more good days than bad. When I go to sleep, he's the person I want to see before I close my eyes, and when I wake up, I always reach for him. He makes my life better for being in it."

He squeezes my arm. "And that's all I want for you. For you to find the kind of happiness that Brando and I have."

"I think I did," I say slowly.

"You'll figure it out," my brother says. "I have faith in you."

"I just have to get out of my own way, first."

thirty-five

. . .

Jason

AMELIA'S BEEN KEEPING her distance. Last night, she went to the Bulldogs game—I watched it on TV with a few of the guys—but I thought she might come over after the game.

But she didn't.

After that day in her office, when I nearly punched out my own teammate, she's kept to herself. She hasn't had lunch with Andrews and the other staffers. They had a two-night trip to DC and, sure, we texted, but there's distance in her messages.

Is she over me? Or is she trying to protect her job?

I'm not offended by the fact that she puts her job first, even before me. She should. We're dating; we don't have anything official. If something happened between us, I want her to have a safety net.

Which is why I have to do this.

The guys are all at morning skate, so the medical offices are empty. Graham and Zac are on the ice, Derek is at his desk, and Amelia is arranging medical supplies in her small office.

I knock on her open door, and she flinches. When she

looks at me, something shutters in her eyes before her face goes carefully blank.

"We can't," she says immediately.

"We can." I limp my way into her office, and then hoist myself up onto the table.

"Jason." Her voice comes out as a whisper.

"I love you."

Her eyes widen, and she looks to the open door.

Cupping her cheek, I force her gaze back to me. "I love you. I want to be with you. And I don't care who knows it."

"But—"

"If you're not in this, if you don't want me, that's fine. I can take it. But if there's even a part of you that wants to be with me, I need you to do me a favor."

Slowly, she blinks. "A favor?"

"Yeah. I need you to sign this." I pick up the folder beside me. "Look this over and see if it's something you can agree to."

"What is it?"

Lifting my chin, I nod to the packet. "Read it over."

She opens the folder, her eyes widening. "Jason, this is—"

"I love you, and I want to be with you, Amelia. I'm in this, and I don't want to hide anymore. I want everyone to know it."

She reads the interpersonal relationship declaration form. My signature is already at the bottom.

"I was offered a job on the coaching staff," I continue. "It involves traveling with the team and working with the guys. We wouldn't be working together directly, per se, but we'd be coworkers."

Swallowing, her eyes dart up to mine, wide as saucers.

"Coworkers and colleagues are allowed to be in relationships together. All we have to do is file with HR."

"That simple?" she breathes.

"That simple." I slide my hand down to the column of her

neck, feeling her pulse flutter beneath my palm. "Sign that form, and we don't have to hide. We can live our lives and be happy."

"I want to be happy," Amelia says softly. "I want to be happy with you."

"We will be." I know it in my bones. "You just have to give us a chance."

She takes a step back, out of my grasp, and my heart stutters to a stop. She turns away, and I think my heart might actually break.

Fuck. I pushed her too far. It's too soon. She's not ready.

But then she goes to her desk, rummaging for a pen, and when she signs her name on the dotted line, I can finally breathe again.

"There," she announces. "We're official."

Slapping the papers onto her desk, she strides across the small office to where I'm sitting. I don't know who reaches for who first, but the next thing I know, she's in my arms, and her mouth is on mine, and all is right with the world.

She's mine, and I'm hers, and there's nothing that can tear us apart.

There's chatter in the hallway outside the office, and we break apart, but we don't go far. Amelia rests her forehead on mine, breathing hard.

"I love you," she whispers.

Happiness blooms deep in my chest, and I blink a few times to keep the moisture in my eyes at bay. "You do?"

"I was scared. So fucking scared." She draws in a shuddery breath. "I was afraid I was into this more than you were. That it didn't mean to you what it does to me."

"I love you. I want a life with you." Kissing her, her soft sigh makes my pulse throb. "Whatever it looks like for us, whether we're traveling three quarters of the year or you want a change of pace, we can do it. I want bagel brunches with your friends and family dinners with your brothers.

Nights out with the guys and quiet nights in. Whatever you want, we'll do it together."

She swallows. "Together," she whispers. It's a promise.

I wrap my hand around her throat again, needing to touch her skin. She covers my hand with hers, her eyes locked on mine.

"We need some ground rules," she says. "We still can't— not at work."

"All our clothes will stay on," I promise. "Can I kiss you? Hold your hand? Take you to lunch?"

Her eyes soften. "Yeah, Jase. You can."

Ducking my head, I kiss her again, and again, and again, until we're both breathless.

There's a knock on the open door, and Amelia jumps, but I don't let her go far. I raise my eyebrows at Derek, who stands in the doorway with a shit-eating grin on his face.

"Glad to see you worked your shit out," he says. "Morning rounds start in five. Better get ready."

He's gone as quickly as he came.

I nod to the packet on her desk. "I better get the paper-work in to the office."

Amelia's cheeks go pink. "Will I see you later?"

"As soon as you'd like." I kiss her quickly, and then hop down onto my good foot. She hands me my crutches and the folder. "I'm off to tell HR."

She winces. "Good luck?"

"It'll go great," I tell her, cupping her cheek. "And if it doesn't, we'll get through it. Together."

We can do anything together.

I head toward the office suite. Jacky, the head of HR, is at her desk, and as I knock on her open door, her eyes widen.

"What can I do for you, McKittrick?"

Passing over the file, she flips it open, and her eyes go even wider.

"You're sure about this?" she asks. I'm not the first player to date a staff member… but soon, I won't be a player anymore. I'll be her peer.

"One hundred and ten percent."

Jacky nods. "Alright, then. I'll get it formalized. You two should be good to go." She pauses. "You deserve someone who makes you happy. Someone who makes you smile like you have been."

"She's pretty fantastic," I agree. "All I want to do is love her. She's finally ready to love me back."

"I wish you a lifetime of happiness," she says, tucking the file into a pile on her desk. "Consider your relationship declared. No fooling around in the training facility, please."

A smirk curves my lips. "We'll do our best."

My errand done, I head down to the dressing room, where the guys are changing out of their kits. All chatter stops when I limp into the room.

"What?" I ask. "Is there something on my face?"

"Oh, Cap," Jenkins says, in a falsetto. "I love you, Cap."

I glare at the kid. "What the fuck did you just say?"

"No, I love you more," Sinclair says, in a high-pitched voice.

Lewis wraps his arms around his shoulders and pretends to make out with himself.

"The fuck is going on here?" My voice comes out as a roar, and Gonzo flinches.

"Shut up, it's cute," Logan says.

My glare narrows on him. "What are you talking about?"

"You and Amelia," Logan says, with a shrug. "You guys ready to finally stop hiding it?"

"What are you talking about?" It sounds hollow. We haven't discussed telling everyone, only that we wouldn't need to keep it a secret.

"Come on, McKittrick," Easton says. "You two have snuck around this place for months."

My mouth drops open. "What?"

"You're always smiling at her," Henry says. "You watch her and smile, and when anyone looks at you, you scowl to cover it. You're totally obvious, bud."

"I've seen her leaving our building, like, seven different times," MacGregor adds. "Doesn't make much sense for her to be over when she lives just next door."

"And her backpack is always inside your front door." Logan shakes his head. "You really make her hide whenever we come over?"

My face heats. "I—we—"

"You can tell us," Larsson says. "You don't have to hide it."

"Yes," Amelia's voice says from behind me. "We're together. And if you say another fucking word about it, the next time you're on my table, you'll cry."

"Yes, ma'am," Larsson says seriously.

She steps up beside me, sliding her hand into mine. "You took too long," she teases, before she kisses me.

The dressing room erupts into cheers and shouts.

"All right, all right, settle down," Coach calls, and we break apart.

Amelia's face is flushed, a smile stretching her face.

"Larsson, you're a healthy scratch tonight," he adds.

The Swede opens his mouth to argue.

"Son, you need to get to the hospital," Coach says. "Vanessa's water just broke. Jacky's called an ambulance, and it'll be here in a few minutes."

Larsson's face goes white. "We're having a baby?"

"Yeah, man," Henry says, slapping his back. "You're having a baby."

And then the dressing room erupts into cheers again.

thirty-six

. . .

Amelia

THE SUPER ROMANTIC moment I envisioned? The one where Jason carries me across the threshold of his apartment and then ravages me?

Kind of foiled by his crutches.

After the game is over, we drive home together. There's no question about where I want to be tonight. I punch the code into the lock, and then hold the door open for him, even though it's his place. Kicking off my shoes, I drop my backpack beside the console table—where it belongs—and all but run to the bedroom.

He takes a bit longer to get there, but when he crosses into his bedroom, I'm already wiggling out of my jeans, my shirt discarded.

Jason launches himself at the bed, landing half on top of me. I erupt into giggles, winding my arms around his neck, and pulling him onto me fully.

"Hi," he whispers, before he kisses me.

I moan into the kiss, one of my hands tangling in his hair. The other slides down his spine to his ass, grabbing hold. Hockey butts are fucking fantastic, round and muscular. I want to bite it.

The kiss is as electric as ever. I don't think I'll ever get tired of him, or the way he tastes, the way he devours me, like I'm his last meal.

He wore a suit to the game—all the players have to, even if they're injured or a healthy scratch—and discarded the jacket as soon as we walked in the door. I like the look of him in a suit. I like it even better when the suit is crumpled on the floor.

My hands move to his buttons, slowly slipping each one free. Halfway down, he gets impatient and yanks, sending little black plastic circles flying. His hips pin me to the bed as he shrugs out of his shirt, throwing it somewhere behind him.

We haven't had sex since his injury. The few times I tried to initiate, he wasn't in the mood, and since things were tense lately…

"Need you," he murmurs against my mouth.

I slip a hand between us, trying to get to his belt buckle. But his hand covers mine, squeezing my fingers.

Pulling back, I try to catch my breath. "I need to talk to you for a moment."

He blinks a few times, and then rises onto his knees.

And immediately winces. He collapses onto his side, grabbing at his shin.

"Yeah. About that," I tell him. "I thought about this a bit, and I think I need to ride you."

"Oh?" A cocky smirk curves across his lips. "You have to, huh?"

"To avoid hurting you more. I think it will be the best position."

Some of the smugness leaves his face. "Oh."

"This way, we both get what we want," I add. "Anything with you on top will set your recovery back. And I'd like you to recover, please."

"Me, too," he says quietly. Seriously. "Whatever you want, Meels."

"Okay." I clap my hands. "Then, pants off."

"You first," he says. Reaching for me, he snaps the elastic of my plain cotton panties. "Off, please."

"But—"

"You're going to ride me," he says. "Sit on my face and ride me, baby."

Oh, he doesn't have to ask me twice.

Wiggling on the bed, I remove my bra and underwear while he works at his belt. The suit pants are pushed haphazardly down his thick thighs, revealing his hard cock, barely contained by boxer briefs.

I rummage in his nightstand for a condom and lube, so we don't have to fumble around later.

Jason rolls over, scooping me into his arms, his front pressed to my back. "Love you," he murmurs, kissing my neck.

"I love you, too." Saying the words isn't as scary as I thought. Instead, I feel… at peace. I love him, and he loves me, and the world didn't end, and I didn't break out in hives. We're officially official with work, so neither of our jobs are at risk.

Our only job now is to be happy. I think I can deal with that.

"Sit on my face, baby," he says. "Let me make you feel good."

I don't hesitate. I turn in the circle of his arms, pressing on his shoulder until he's flat on his back, and then I'm climbing up to the pillows. Straddling his head, I hover in position, my heart thudding loudly in my chest.

His hands on my hips pull me down roughly, until his mouth brushes my pussy, and then I finally relax. This is where I belong. In this bed, with this man. This is where I want to be.

He licks and sucks at my center, and Jason's lips are soft, his rough stubble scraping the inside of my thighs. I absolutely love it. He eats me like he's starving, like he's been salivating for this moment.

My thighs start to shake, and even holding onto the headboard for support, I'm trembling.

"Let go," he murmurs against my pussy. "Don't fight it."

So, I close my eyes, throw my shoulders back, and ride the waves of pleasure. Bright white light erupts behind my eyelids as I crest the peak.

Jason licks me clean, rubbing his hands over my thighs as I come down.

When it gets to be too much, I lift myself off of him, collapsing onto my side.

He looks entirely too smug, his mouth glistening with the evidence of my desire. Turning his head to look at me, he reaches a hand out, and I slide my fingers into his.

"Good?" he asks.

"Shut up. You know you're good at that." My snap is teasing, affectionate.

His eyes crinkle when he smiles. "I was asking if you're good. You're okay?"

"Yeah, Jase. I'm good."

He squeezes my fingers, and as I catch my breath, I drink in the sight of him. His cut shoulders, strong chest, and defined abs are as muscular as ever. If he retires, if he takes this new job, will he soften a bit? I kind of like the idea of him with a soft belly. I like the muscles, sure. But I just like him. Whatever his muscle tone and body fat percentage, I'll still love him just the same.

Shifting in the bed, I straddle his waist, his condom-covered cock directly in front of my clit. I rut against him, rubbing myself along the underside of his shaft, and he lets out a shuddery breath.

"Amelia," he groans, his hands moving to my hips.

"Yes?" I tease, my lips curving into a satisfied smile.

"You're killing me."

"Oh, we can't have that now." Rising onto my knees, I position his cock at my entrance, slowly sinking down onto him.

The groan he lets out rattles through me.

"I had a thought."

He grunts. "Oh?"

"One benefit of the vasectomy," I tell him, breathing hard. "You can come inside me all you want."

Buried within me, his cock jerks, and he lets out a hiss through his teeth as his eyes darken, the pupils nearly fully eclipsing the chocolate irises. "You'd let me?"

"After the procedure," I hasten to add.

Jason wraps his hand around my throat, tugging gently until I'm sprawled across his chest. He kisses me, hard, demanding.

When I'm finally about to burst out of my skin, I force myself upright, and then I start to ride him. His hands clench my hips, helping me rise and sink back onto his cock, and I love the delicious pressure that's sure to bruise.

I love *him*.

Pleasure barrels into me like a freight truck, and it doesn't take long before he shouts, his cock pulsing inside me.

Breathing hard, I collapse onto the mattress beside him, and he pulls me into his arms. I rest my head on his chest, the slight friction of the hair there abrading my cheek. My fingers go to the divot between his abs, the dips and grooves of his body a soothing texture.

"I think you should take the job." The words come out before I even think about them.

Jason hums. "You do?"

"If you want it. It means we'd still travel together. We'd work together." I swallow. "If you don't… we can look for another job. Or you can take a few months or a year off."

"I want the job," he says firmly. "I don't know if I want to be a head bench boss one day, but I like the idea of coaching the younger guys. I already did it for years as captain."

"And we'll stay in Boston?"

"For as long as you want," he says. "If Brandon gets traded, would you follow him?"

I wince. "Probably. Not him specifically, but Ty. And Ainsley."

"She's such a cutie. I can't wait to spoil her rotten."

Looking up at him, I find a fond smile on his face. "You'd spoil her?"

"She's your niece. It's my right as your partner to shower her with gifts and feed her sugar before giving her back to your brothers." He chuckles. "My siblings live too far away. I like my nieces and nephews, but I don't have the same relationship with them that you do with Ainsley. Hell, I barely talk to my siblings."

"That can change. We can spend more time with them now that you won't be playing."

His shoulder lifts beneath me as he shrugs. "Maybe. I'm good with Ty and Brando, though. Family is about the people you choose to keep in your life." Jason blows out a breath. "When we go to the lake this summer, you'll come with me?"

"You couldn't keep me away."

"You say that now," he mutters. "They might scare you off."

I set my hand over his heart, the reassuring thudding settling my nerves. "Nothing will scare me off. Not your family. Not your teammates. Not even your stinky hockey gear."

He laughs. "Good. 'Cause I'd kind of like to keep you."

"Oh, Jase," I murmur. "You've already got me."

epilogue

. . .

Jason

"WELL, BOYS," MacGregor says loudly. "We've lost another good one."

There are jeers from the twenty-two other players assembled in front of him.

"McKittrick's gone and gotten himself all settled down and boring. He's hanging up the jersey and pads, but he's still got his skates."

"Hey, watch it," I call out. "I might make you do suicides tomorrow."

MacGregor laughs. "Seriously, Cap. I am so happy you found this new venture. Even if it means you'll torture us every day on the ice, this new job couldn't have went to a better guy. We're glad you're still with the team. You'll always be one of us. A brother."

"Hear, hear," Gonzo calls out.

My eyes sting, and I blink a few times, trying to force back the wave of emotions threatening to overtake me.

Beside me, Amelia reaches for my hand, lacing our fingers together. She's by my side. I know she'll always be by my side.

Going out on a career-ending injury is not how I wanted

my fourteen years in the NHL to end. I wanted to lift the Cup, to bring the championship back to Boston for the first time in way too many years.

I didn't get a choice in the matter, though. And now, looking back, I wouldn't have it any other way.

My leg is still healing, but I'm back to walking on two legs and strengthening the muscles every day. My NHL contract technically doesn't end until June thirtieth, so even though I've played my last game and have no intention of returning to the ice, I can still use the team's PT staff. Come July first, though, I'll have to find someone else—someone outside of the arena.

Luckily, Amelia has friends and colleagues everywhere, and she set me up with a friend of hers from DPT school. Charles is a laid-back dude, who could probably snap me like a twig if he wanted—and that's saying something, considering my size.

It was important to both me and Amelia that she didn't handle my PT. Our relationship wouldn't survive it. I can bitch about Charles torturing me all I want, but at the end of the session, we go our separate ways. Now that Amelia lives with me, there's not as much separation.

She moved in a few days after the team's post-season run came to an abrupt end. We were swept by Washington in the second round, dashing all our hopes and dreams.

But not all of *mine*.

Because I'm finally dreaming again. I've thought about a future post-hockey, and yes, it's scary, but it's also so freeing.

I'm still not ready to think about marriage. I rushed into it the first time. I won't make that mistake again. Amelia and I talk about it, and she's not pushing for a ring, either. We're taking it day-by-day, one step at a time.

The team is gathered for my official retirement party. It's a full family affair. All the support staff joined us, and those with partners and children brought them. Tyler, Brandon, and

Ainsley are here, too. Most retirement parties aren't nearly as inclusive, but it was important to me that everyone who wanted to come was invited.

If there's one thing I'm most proud of, it's the inclusive and accepting locker room we built and sustained. We're all a family, and with the long hours and constant travel, it's easy to get snippy with each other. At the end of the day, though, it all comes down to one thing, and that's sharing the sport we love with the city we love.

Boston is my home. The last eight years here were amazing, and I wouldn't trade them for the world. Yes, there were some difficult times. But it doesn't discount how awesome the city is. And it doesn't take away from all the personal growth I made over the years.

I am who I am because of hockey. Because of the Boston Grizzlies. And because of Amelia.

Her love gets me through the bad days. She supports me in so many ways. Sometimes, I think she doesn't even recognize how much she does. And I do my best to support her right back. To show her each and every day just how much I love her.

My thoughts on marriage aside, there's no denying that I see a future for us. Whether or not it's a legal relationship, there's no changing how I feel about her. I'm committed to her. To us. To our future. Together. We're partners in every sense of the world.

As the party drags on, Amelia and I mingle with our friends. Teammates. Coworkers. Come Monday morning, everything changes. I'll be in a position of authority over the guys I think of as my brothers. It's a step beyond being captain.

I'm ready for it, though. And I already know who the next guy to wear the C is.

MacGregor is talking to his sister Hailey and Logan, who looks as smitten with her as ever. Catching his eye, I wave him over, and he threads his way through the party to where I'm standing near the drinks table.

"What's up, Cap?" he says, tossing his water bottle from one hand to the other, and then back again.

My smile is tinged with sadness. "I'm not your captain anymore."

He shakes his head. "You'll always be our captain. Except when you're our coach." MacGregor gives a cheeky grin, looking entirely too pleased with himself. "Unless you'd like us to call you Coach Captain."

"Oh, fuck off," I groan. "I wanted to say something nice to you, but if you're going to be a dick…"

"Aww, you like me," he teases. "Tell me."

Blowing out a breath, I meet his eyes. "I think you should be the next captain of the Boston Grizzlies."

MacGregor blinks a few times. "What the *fuck*?"

His shout draws attention from the other partygoers, and I shake my head to hide my smile.

"I'm recommending you to Coach Turner for the open captain position."

"Me? You're nuts."

"Maybe so. I still think it should be you."

He gapes at me, his mouth hanging open.

"You've led this team for the last few months. When I went out, you took over seamlessly, leading the boys when I couldn't."

MacGregor frowns. "But I couldn't win you a Cup."

"And that's okay. We did our best. It wasn't our fault that Washington was simply better."

Although since they went on to the Stanley Cup Finals, I guess it doesn't hurt as much as if they'd lost in the Conference Finals.

"We can't win every year," I continue. "It just means we'll work harder next season. And I think you should be the one to lead the team."

He cocks his head, clearly thinking it over.

"We don't need an answer yet. Enjoy your offseason, consider all your options." I clap his shoulder. "But you should say yes. It's a lot of work, but it's so fucking rewarding."

MacGregor swallows. "I know I'm not the most social guy..."

"Yeah, so maybe you'll have to go out a little bit more," I concede. Considering he never goes out, anything more would be an improvement. "But being captain is more than being out at the bar with the guys. It's about the team as a whole gelling, and being able to lead when we're down three nothing with two minutes left. Or when we're on a losing streak and nobody can get their heads out of their asses. It's the bad as much as it's the good. I don't want to scare you off. It's a lot of fucking work. But going out there with the C on your chest… There's nothing like it."

"I'll think about it," MacGregor promises. He clears his throat, nodding behind me. "Incoming."

I turn to find Amelia approaching, Ainsley on her hip. Tyler is across the room, talking to Andrews and Joaquin.

"Hey, you," I say as she draws near. I reach for the baby's chubby fist, and she wraps her tiny fingers around my pinky. My heart melts. "Having fun?"

"Oh, she's having a blast," Amelia reports. Ainsley is ten and a half months old, and already the belle of the ball. She was passed around the party all day, and even Sinclair and Jenkins showed interest in the baby.

Between her and Leo, Larsson's son, it seems like everyone has baby fever. Easton's wife Mel is pregnant again, and Henry's wife Audrey is talking to Vanessa and Jacky about strollers.

Not me. Amelia and I are happily child-free, and I had the vasectomy to prove it.

There's no doubt in my mind that she's the one for me,

and that we're in this for the long haul. We're in a good place. Sure, there's a lot of change on the horizon for us. Moving in together was a big step. Switching from player to coach is sure to be emotional.

But with her by my side, I can do anything. She makes me more confident in myself and my decision. She believes in me, so how can I not?

Amelia hands me the baby, and I cuddle Ainsley in my arms. She squirms closer, burying her face in my neck, and I rove my hand over her small back. The baby loves me, and not just because I babysit her every other Thursday afternoon while Tyler is at work.

In a few weeks, we're going to the lake house to meet my family. My brother and sisters will be there with my nieces and nephews. It'll be a *very* loud week. Rewarding, too, though.

I told them bits and pieces about Amelia. We did a few video chats. But it's not the same as meeting them in person. We invited Tyler to join us, but since Brandon has a stretch of home games, he wants to be home with his husband. I don't blame him. Maybe next year, he'll join us if our trip lines up with an away series.

We see them regularly, and not just through our windows. Most Sunday mornings, Tyler has us over for brunch, and although we've invited him over multiple times, he insists on hosting Friday night dinners at his place, too. We go to nearly all of Brandon's games, now that hockey season is over, and it'll be a jam-packed summer of baseball.

It's funny. It's not the life I imagined for myself. It's certainly not the life I had a year ago. But it's one I wouldn't change for the world.

Amelia leans close, hugging me and her niece at the same time.

"I love you," she whispers, her lips brushing mine.

"I love you, more."

———

Want more of Amelia and Jason? Here's a bonus chapter five years later.

Does Logan ever ask out his best friend's little sister? Read his story in *Defenseless*. They're both virgins, and he's been waiting for her. When their ten-year high school reunion rolls around, he's not going to pass up the opportunity to relive the prom night they never got.

what's next?

Thank you for reading *Body Check*. I hope you enjoyed reading this book as much as I enjoyed writing it!

Does Logan ever ask out his best friend's little sister? Read his story in *Defenseless*. They're both virgins, and he's been waiting for her. When their ten-year high school reunion rolls around, he's not going to pass up the opportunity to relive the prom night they never got.

Want to see how it all started? Read *Puck Me Twice*, where autistic hockey player convinces the one night stand that took his virginity, and now works for his hockey team, to give him a second chance — as her *fake* boyfriend.

Want some heartwarming holiday fun? Check out *Home for the Holidays*, a Chanukah novella featuring goaltender Jake Lewis and nuclear physicist Rachel, his new roommate... and his brother's ex.

afterword

Thank you for reading *Body Check*. This book is my baby and I absolutely love it to pieces.

Reviews are more important than readers realize. If you liked this book, please leave me a review!

Join my newsletter to stay in the loop! Lots of unfunny quips, unsuccessful attempts at wit, and general grouching about the writing process.

xoxo,

Allie

about the author

Allie is a queer and AuDHD writer with a hyper-fixation on inclusivity and representation. She loves the color purple, Michigan football, the Detroit Lions, and the Boston Bruins. When she's not absorbed by a book, she likes to spend time with her nephews.

A San Diego, CA native now residing in South Carolina, she is allergic to the cold, rain, snow, and mosquitos.

also by allie lasky

Meet the Neurospicy Book Club in The Thought of You, where grumpy Johanna finds out she's autistic… because her happy-go-lucky new roomie (and reformed playboy ex-football player) has to tell her.

———

For more Own Voices, try Spark: A Chanukah Novella, where neurodivergent Arielle and her childhood friend Asher finally connect after two decades of missed chances.

———

Want to see how it all started? Read <u>The Game Plan</u> to meet sweet cinnamon roll football player Miles and the feisty sorority girl who stole his heart.